Wild Irish Heart

W0006188

TRICIA O'MALLEY

"Maireann lá go ruaig ach maireann an grá go huaigh."
A day lasts until it's chased away but love lasts until the grave.

Chapter One

THE PING OF the doorbell startled Keelin O'Brien from her daydream of chartering a dive boat through the Great Barrier Reef. Blinking, she shoved herself up from her messy desk and padded quietly in her Irish cottage socks to the door. Peering through the hole, she saw that it was Frank, her overly friendly mailman.

"Hi, Frank," Keelin said as she eased the door open, careful to hide her clutter from his view.

"Hi, Keelin. I've got a special package for you today," Frank said. "International!"

"Really? I haven't ordered anything. How interesting." Keelin signed for the package and Frank raised his eyebrows at her. Keelin knew that he expected her to open the package in front of him.

"Thanks, Frank. Gotta run!" Keelin shut the door with her foot and examined the small package as she wandered towards her kitchen. The cheerful blue of her kitchen walls contrasted with the pile of dishes in her sink. A small window with soft yellow curtains allowed a ray of sunlight to pick up the layer of dust on her sideboard. With a sigh, Keelin made a mental note to clean.

Brushing a pile of papers aside, Keelin sat at her table and looked at the package. Rectangular-shaped and wrapped in butcher paper, it wasn't the typical international envelope found at the post office. Twine wove around the package and what looked like an honest-to-God wax seal closed the twine. Keelin's name and address were written in a deep brown ink, the handwriting a beautiful old calligrapher style. Keelin squinted at the return address and remembered her reading glasses, tucked in her shirt.

Interesting, Keelin thought as she examined the address more closely. The address was smudged. It seemed almost deliberate. Keelin wondered why she suspected that it was deliberate. Only one word was easily readable: Ireland.

Keelin lifted the package and gingerly broke the seal. An image flashed into her head. Flames slicing into the night. Voices chanting. A midnight-blue cove that glowed from within. And eyes. A sharp, crystal-blue pair of eyes stared at her through the flames.

Keelin gasped and dropped the package. Her heart pounded quickly and she tried out some of the deep-breathing techniques that she had learned in yoga. Though her hands trembled, Keelin shook her head and laughed at herself. Her mother always sighed at what she termed

"Keelin's Little Fancies" and clucked that Keelin would never find a man if she was always daydreaming. Keelin wished that these images were just daydreams or the result of an overly creative brain. Unfortunately, Keelin's talents ran more to the science side of things than the creative, daydreamer type. Yet, Keelin never knew how to describe the images she would see when she touched certain things.

Things? Who was she kidding? Keelin thought. It didn't just happen with objects. It happened with people, animals, and even places. She had recently started to wonder if she needed to take her mother's not-so-gentle advice to go see a therapist. Keelin's gut told her that a therapist would do little to shed light on her problems. She'd learned long ago to shelter herself and to keep these images that flooded her brain quiet. Living in Massachusetts had implemented in her a healthy fear of the repercussions of being different, if the history of the Salem Witch Trials indicated anything.

She held the package and took a deep breath before she immersed herself back in the image. This time, she focused on the feelings it brought.

Dark images slashed at her. A fishing village at night. A lone dog wandering a hill. A man tying a fishing line. As Keelin waded through the images she decided that there was a feeling of foreboding, yet also of homecoming, that threaded through the images. It wasn't evil, yet there was a sense of stepping over a threshold.

It was almost as if she was being pushed away and pulled in. Her fingers trembled as she peeled back the paper. In some respects, she had been waiting for this. There had always been something in her life left unsaid – undiscovered even. Keelin wondered if this was finally her answer.

A small book lay nestled in the paper. A rich brown leather cover, creased with age, and with hand stitching at the binding, encased the yellowed pages. Keelin marveled over the beauty of the simple craftsmanship. No words or symbols marred the soft leather, yet years of scratches from use had weathered the cover to a perfect patina.

The book seemed to speak volumes without a word on its cover.

This book was old. Really old. Keelin wondered if she needed gloves to touch it. A book like this belonged in a museum, she thought. She gently opened the cover and gasped at the pages. These were vellum pages. Her hands shook as the enormity of the delicacy and strength of this book struck her. Keelin had known the book was old but writing on vellum dated back to the Book of Kells days. This was a book that was not to be taken lightly. Who had sent such a gift to her?

Keelin suspected she knew the source of this gift. The real question was: why now?

A folded piece of paper that was tied with the same twine and matching seal as the wrapping lay tucked in the front of the cover. Keelin gently pulled it out and unfolded it.

The words struck her like a punch to the gut.

It is time.

Keelin stared at the letter in shock. In recognition. She tucked her strawberry-blonde hair behind her ear. Her socialite mother carefully tinted the red from her hair, sniffing, "It's too Irish." But Keelin secretly loved her hair color and always refused to have it dyed when her mother's second-favorite stylist discreetly suggested the change each month.

It is time.

The words bored into her brain. Had she known this was coming? She held the letter up to her face. It smelled faintly of lavender and something deeper. Smoky, almost. Visions of a moonlit cove, a boat, and the promise of lust and love flashed through her mind.

It is time.

Keelin held the book and marveled at the beauty of the detailing. She closed her eyes and inhaled the scent of the worn leather. The book seemed to warm to her touch and a feeling of love spread through her arms and curled its way through her core. She caught a glimpse of an old woman gathering herbs on a sloping hill near the water. Her sudden insight confirmed her suspicion. This was her maternal grandmother's book. Her grandmother lived in the hills of Ireland, just north of a small fishing village on the southernmost peninsula of Ireland. Reported to be crazy and aloof, Keelin had had little contact with her. Keelin's mother had insisted on moving to the States before Keelin was born and was proud to raise her daughter on Boston's reputable Beacon Hill. They had never returned to Ireland.

She had often wondered why her mother had refused to discuss her upbringing with Keelin. At the time, she had put it down to her mom's obsession with pedigree and socialite parties. There wasn't much place for a poor Irish upbringing amongst the wealth of her mother's friends. Now Keelin wondered what vital details she may have missed about her mother's life before Boston.

The book seemed to call to her. Keelin traced her fingers over the soft leather. She picked it up and the image of blue eyes popped into her head again. This time a small thrill of heat curled through her.

"Whoa, this is a little ridiculous." Keelin laughed and got up. She needed to pace. Two thoughts raced through her mind. The first was that her grandmother was dead. The second was that this was a book of power.

Keelin needed answers and there was only one blonde socialite that had them.

She pulled on knee-high brown boots over leggings that hugged generous hips, threw on a long fair-isle cardigan, and picked up the book. Keelin dug in her closet for a wool scarf and gently wrapped the book before tucking it in her leather satchel. It was time to hunt down her mother. Then she would deal with the implications of the book.

Chapter Two

MARGARET GRAINNE O'BRIEN lived in a two-story brownstone in the coveted Beacon Hill neighborhood of downtown Boston. Keelin enjoyed the cobblestone streets and the cherry blossom trees in the spring. She hated the severe lack of parking and the miniscule living spaces that the high-rent neighborhood offered. Wondering, again, why anyone would pay an obscene amount of money to live in seven hundred square feet of space with one parking spot, Keelin rang her mother's bell.

"Keelin, darling! What are you doing here?" Margaret asked. A coolly lovely blonde in her late forties, she was dressed for tea in a pale gray cocktail suit with a deep pink shirt. Pearls winked at her ears and a leather watch peeked discreetly from her sleeve.

Margaret ushered Keelin in and began making distressed noises.

"Keelin Grainne. Are you wearing leggings outside of the house again?" Margaret asked.

"Mom. Stop. Everyone wears leggings. And my sweater is long. They are like tights but with even more coverage." Keelin rolled her eyes and stomped to her mother's front room. Graceful arched windows boasted a view of fashionable shops. Keelin settled on the settee and actively hated the room. Everything was white and gold. Too much opulence, she thought.

"Mom. We need to talk." Keelin reached into her bag to pull out the book.

"You're pregnant! I knew it. I knew that Todd was bad news. What were you thinking?"

"Whoa. What? No! Mom, ugh, God, just stop. Gross. I never slept with Todd to begin with. You set me up with him, which should have told you that he was not a good match for me. Would you please just stop with trying to set me up?" Keelin said. It was a constant aggravation for her. Margaret enjoyed arranging blind dates with the sons of the town's elite. Keelin loved her too much to embarrass her and ditch out on the dates. Inevitably, every Todd, Chad, and Spence she dated failed to get her juices flowing. Idly, she wondered if she even had any juices anymore. It had been so long since she had truly been passionate about anything except her work.

"Thank God. I would hate to tell Shirley that her son was a jerk. Now, why are you here in the middle of the day? Shouldn't you be working on an application?" Margaret said. She was referring to Keelin's internship applications. Keelin had been working for the Boston Aquarium for the past few years and had wanted to branch out for a while. Her secret dream was to finish her master's degree in marine biology and to work on a research-and-dive team. She hoped to get aboard a research vessel as an intern over the summer.

Keelin decided to go for impact. She reached into her satchel and withdrew her scarf-wrapped bundle.

"Keelin, when will you get rid of that ugly scarf? It is so Irish," Margaret said, her disdain evident.

Silently, Keelin unwrapped the bundle and placed the book on the table, watching her mother closely. Margaret's eyes widened slightly and then returned to normal.

"Why, whatever is this old book? Is this for school?" Margaret asked. Keelin noticed that her normally pale mother's cheeks were flushed and her hand played a *tap-tap-tap* rhythm on the Eastlake side table.

"Mom. You know what this is. I need answers," Keelin said.

"I have no idea what you mean. It is an old book. Lovely, actually. I see books like this in the antique shops. You should place it on display," Margaret said. She refused to meet Keelin's eyes and glanced quickly at her watch.

"Darling, I am so sorry, but I have to meet Mrs. Thatcher for tea. We are going over plans for the book club's charity fundraiser. I mustn't be late," Margaret said as she stood.

"I don't think so. Sit down," Keelin said.

"Keelin. What is wrong with you? Do not speak to me like that." Margaret stood her ground. You could take the Irish out of Ireland, Keelin mused.

"This is your mother's book. My grandmother. I can feel it. I know it. This arrived today. Does this mean she is dead? Do you even talk to her anymore?" The questions tumbled out. Keelin didn't mean to sound accusatory but the old bitterness welled up in her throat. She'd always hated how Margaret had isolated her from learning about her Irish roots.

Sighing, Margaret walked to the wet bar and poured herself a whiskey, neat. Shocked, Keelin watched as her mild-mannered mother downed it in one gulp.

"I knew that this time would arrive," Margaret said. Her shoulders were tense and she stayed focused on the wet bar.

"Um, yeah. No kidding. The letter said, 'it is time,'" Keelin said. "Care to elaborate?"

"This is the reason that I left your father, the town, and have never returned to Ireland." Margaret's back was still turned. "I had hoped this day would never come."

Chapter Three

OKAY, DRAMA QUEEN," Keelin said. "Let's bring it down a notch. This is all a little much for me."

A small smile flitted over Margaret's face as she turned to face Keelin. "You were always so irreverent. Part of me has always wished that I could be the same."

Keelin was shocked. Her mom admired what she so chastised? Interesting, she thought.

"If you'll excuse me, I need a moment to cancel my meeting. Then I will discuss that…that book with you," Margaret said as she strode purposefully from the room. Her back, ramrod straight, radiated determination and fortitude as usual. Keelin automatically straightened her shoulders. Just looking at her mother made her feel like a slob.

Idly, she let her hands trace the book. The supple leather seemed to warm to her touch again.

"Let's go," Margaret said. Keelin jumped and gasped.

"Mother! I didn't know you owned jeans!"

"Well, yes, if I ever went for a walk in the woods, I would need a pair, wouldn't I?" Margaret's tidy blue jeans were tucked into Hunter boots and her thick cardigan was buttoned perfectly. A plaid scarf topped her outfit and screamed "Ralph Lauren chic."

"Woods? What woods are you walking in, Mom?" Keelin asked.

"Well, the Common, of course. They have lovely trees."

Keelin had to laugh. Only her mother would refer to the manicured lawns of the Boston Common as "the woods."

"Okay, Mom. Let's go for a walk." Keelin tucked the book into her satchel and gathered her cardigan. She watched as her mother gathered her keys from the gold Hermès dish by the door, and made sure the doormat was aligned just so.

How had she come from such a woman? This wasn't a new thought to Keelin. Messy, disobedient, and opinionated, Keelin felt like she was a constant disappointment to her polite and reserved mother. She often felt like she was playing a role when her mother invited her to the society's most elite functions. Silk dresses and being seen mattered little to Keelin when she could bury her head in a book or hear some great local music. Her mom knew what every spoon and fork meant in a table setting, while Keelin preferred cider and a greasy burger from the local bar. For all their differences, a pure, strong love ran between them. It had been just the two of them for so long. She couldn't fault her mother for wanting the best for her.

As was typical of a Friday afternoon, the Common bustled with activity. The pulse of the city seemed to beat there, as people from all walks of life flowed from the stairwells of the T, dispersing into the green of the Common and weaving between the ponds and trees. It never failed to interest her, the people she found here, Keelin thought. Keelin had spent many an afternoon thinking about the lives of those who walked past her picnic blanket. She often played a game without really knowing why. Keelin would guess the ailments of strangers. She had no way of confirming how or why she knew what she did but she did it without thinking. Cancer, cold sore, cough, diabetes, sprained wrist…images flashed through her head along with emotions. It was like a game show where she had no way of knowing if she was a winner.

Keelin walked quietly beside her mother and listened as she rattled off the prices of the apartments that lined the Common. She knew all of this already, yet allowed her mother to talk. Margaret had a tendency to talk real estate when she was nervous. Eventually, they wound their way to a stone bench overlooking a small pond. Keelin idly watched a mother help her toddler feed the ducks.

"What do you know of Grace's Cove?" Margaret asked.

"Well, I know that it is a small town on the water in Southern Ireland. I know that you grew up there and didn't like the village lifestyle. I've googled it and the pictures are stunning. It really looks like a beautiful place to live. And, I'd love to get out on the water there. Those cliffs are incredible! I imagine there is a ton to study," Keelin said.

"Yes, well, I'm not surprised you like the water so much, as your father was a fisherman," Margaret said.

"Yes, so you've said," Keelin said. She was surprised that her mother had brought him up. A source of bitterness between them, Keelin knew little of her father and Margaret rarely spoke of him.

"I understand that I made a decision to remove him from your life, Keelin, however, it was in your best interests. And look at the life that I gave you. I had my reasons," Margaret said.

Keelin stayed silent. She'd heard this refrain before. What was the point of arguing the past?

Margaret sighed. "I suppose it is time for you to know more about your heritage."

"Yes, that would be nice," Keelin said dryly as she picked at some fuzz on her sweater.

"I loved your father, deeply," Margaret said.

Keelin gasped. She had always assumed that she was an "oops" and her father was a passionate night in passing.

"Oh, Keelin, we were so young and in love. He was working to be a commercial fisherman and had plans to go to Dublin to open a commercial fishing business. That, or start a boat tour company. Either way, you couldn't keep him from the water if you had tried. Sean had quite the big dreams. He…he didn't know about you until I had left. I never told him. Leaving Ireland was one of the hardest things that I have done."

Keelin stared in shock at her mother. Margaret's cheeks were flushed, yet there was a stubborn tilt to her chin. There would be no questioning of her past decisions.

"But, how could you not tell him?"

"He ran from me. He left me, Keelin. When I found out about you, I knew that the only thing that mattered was that I give you a chance at a normal life."

"But, Mom, didn't you miss him? What was so bad that you had to leave?" Keelin asked.

"I missed him terribly. I still do. I see pieces of him in you. We aren't the same people anymore though, and that time has passed. Let me tell you about the history of Grace's Cove."

Keelin nodded and kept silent. This was the most she had ever gotten out of her mother and she wouldn't let her big mouth sidetrack Margaret from giving her the information she so desperately craved.

"Have you heard of the famous pirate queen, Grace O'Malley?"

"Of course; she is legendary throughout Ireland. She was notorious for her fierceness in battle. I know she married twice and had several children. She was famous for being ruthless, yet at the same time is credited with preserving much of Gaelic history."

"Absolutely, and she was a woman that knew her own mind. Did you know that Grainne is the Celtic name for

Grace?" Margaret asked. Both Keelin and Margaret's middle name was Grainne.

"I did not," Keelin said.

"Almost all of the women of a particular bloodline in Grace's Cove carry that name. It isn't because of the town name. It is because our bloodline is that of Grace O'Malley."

"Shut up." Keelin was thrilled. She was related to a famous pirate queen? How cool was that?

"Keelin, do not say shut up."

"Sorry, Mom."

"Yes, you are a descendant of Grace O'Malley, for whom Grace's Cove is named. Your grandmother has a direct connection and experiences the effects of it."

"Of what? I don't understand. Is ol' Grandma a pirate or something?" Keelin asked.

Margaret smiled. "No, not quite. Grace was rumored to have powers other than her formidable ones as a pirate queen. Some say magick. Others say a healer. Others point to almost a psychic ability to predict potential threats. It isn't really known what all surrounded Grace, yet almost all will agree she had a level of power."

Keelin began to nervously pick at her nails. She pulled at a loose hangnail and winced as blood came to the surface. Without thinking she covered it with her hand and the wound slowly faded.

"The cove itself is rumored to be enchanted. Almost no one will go there. Well, aside from your grandmother. And a few others. I've gone there. I never will again."

"Wait. What. You're kidding me, right?" Keelin said. She pictured the stunning images of the cove that she had seen on Google. It was impossible to think that people wouldn't spend time there.

"The Irish are a very superstitious people, Keelin. Nobody will go there. People who do are often swept out to sea or injured on the rocks. They say that the moon won't reflect off the water there – yet at times the sea glows from within."

"Okay, Mom, stop. There are perfectly plausible explanations for these things. Oftentimes coves have whirlpools or riptides that will pull people out to sea. As for glowing from within, there are certain types of phosphorous plankton that can create a glowing illusion on the water. I'm sure it is all just a superstition," Keelin said.

Margaret smiled and shook her head. "You're so smart. And typically, I would agree with you, had I not seen the power for myself. I won't go back there. My mother went into the cove regularly and never had a problem but she had her own way of doing so."

"Mom, why is it named Grace's Cove? What is the connection?"

"Well, it is rumored that Grace O'Malley hid the Chalice of Ardagh there and that the one in the national museum is a companion piece to the real chalice."

"What! Mother. No. That is insane. The Chalice of Ardagh is part of Irish national pride. If that were true there would have been expeditions. Divers would have found it. The cove is not that big."

"Oh, there have been expeditions. Many. They've all failed. The government got sick of spending money on it and now dismisses it as a silly superstition and warns people against going to the dangerous waters of the cove. The official statement is that there is a powerful current that will sweep you out to sea. The unofficial statement is that it is cursed."

Keelin stared at the pond. The ducks swam lazily, picking at the offerings of bread. The science side of her mind concurred with the official reason for the cove's problems. The "other" side of her that stayed awake at night with visions, hummed. Her mom's words were like a balm of truth to her soul. Conflicted, Keelin rubbed her hands together, not seeing that her nail wound had completely healed.

"How come Grandma could go there? How does the book play into all this? Is this why you left?" Keelin had so many questions.

"Your grandmother and I had a difficult relationship. It was one of the reasons that I left with you. Her plans for you didn't coincide with my plans. I needed to give you a chance at a normal life," Margaret said again, nervously twisting a gold band around her right hand.

"Um, what? How am I supposed to respond to that? Can you just say it straight?" Keelin liked to work with facts.

Margaret sighed. Her twisting movements became faster. Keelin reached out and put her hand on her mother's.

"Mom, just say it."

18

"That book is your grandmother's. She was constantly devoted to it. She carried it everywhere and was always writing carefully in it. Your grandmother is famous throughout Ireland as a wise woman – a healer. There are those that claim she is a witch. I don't believe that. Yet, I've seen her cure people where modern medicine was unable to. She never let me see the book. She told me it was for my daughter and that I had other gifts. I never planned to get pregnant, so I didn't think about leaving Grace's Cove until I was surprised with you. I couldn't let you grow up with such nonsense. What kind of life would that be for you? People only come to healers if they need their services and healers are often shunned in other places. Healers are the focus of constant whispered gossip. With Fiona as my mother, no matter if we went into a pub or a store – someone always talked. The more religious members of the town would switch directions and cross themselves when we walked by. I just wanted a normal upbringing for you, not like the one that I had. I just wanted the best for you. You have to understand. I gave up my everything. My love, my family, my life so that you could be a normal child. And I still fear that I was never able to give you what you needed. She may have been right."

"Mom. I had a great childhood. It's fine," Keelin said quickly. Too quickly.

"Keelin. No, you didn't." Margaret sighed deeply and clutched Keelin's hand. "You had constant visions, daydreams, and night terrors. You would scare the crap out of our friends when you told them they were sick or what would happen with a family member. And that time that you healed our cat that was hit by a car? You were five. Five! You are not normal and there is nothing that I can do to change that. You are touched with something special. Maybe it is time that I embrace this and do what I can to help you. You'll never find happiness if you don't address this."

Keelin was surprised to feel her cheeks were wet with tears. She hadn't felt herself start crying but it was like a part of her heart had cracked open. Her walls had been up for so long that she rarely thought of her childhood or how difficult her life could be at times. Her mother knew. She saw all of it. All of her struggles as a child. Her difficulty in relationships because Keelin always knew too much. She had a tendency to scare people without meaning to. It had taught her to pick her relationships wisely and to keep her bonds tenuous.

"Oh, honey, I'm so sorry. Don't cry. I always knew this day would come, though I wish your grandmother had picked a less dramatic way of doing this, without sending that book to you. I love you no matter what. Even if you may have a touch of Grace O'Malley's "power" in you. I mean, would you really be Irish if you didn't have a little extra something in you?" Margaret cracked a small smile.

"Mom, can you heal people? Do you have the same thing that I do?" Keelin was eager for answers.

"No, Keelin, I do not. My strengths come in other ways. I can read people's emotions from a mile away. Why do you think that I can close a sale in a heartbeat?" Margaret smiled her ferocious realtor's smile. Keelin nodded. It made sense, after all. A single mom straight off the boat from Ireland would have had to have an extra "something" to rocket to the top of the real estate empire in Boston.

"So, what does this mean for me? I don't know what to do." Keelin stared at the book.

"I don't want you to go. I really don't. In fact, I am terrified that I will lose you. But, if you want to learn about yourself, you may have to go to Ireland. If you want to ignore it and carry on here – I completely support that," Margaret said eagerly.

Keelin laughed. She knew her mother wanted to keep her safe, under her watch. The book hummed in her lap.

"I think that I might have to go."

Chapter Four

KEELIN WALKED HOME, the book warm against her side. Her mother had held her close when they parted and whispered how sorry she was. Keelin mulled over all that she had learned on the walk through the busy rush-hour street traffic. She felt like there was a small pressure building deep in her stomach and she was unsure if it was from fear or excitement. Possibilities began to snake through her mind.

Once home, Keelin fixed a pot of black tea, one of the few things she was capable of making well, and curled up on her couch with the book. She blew softly on the tea that steamed from her favorite flower mug. The pressure built in her stomach and she got the eerie feeling that she was staring at her destiny.

"Now or never," Keelin murmured. Careful to set the tea far away from the book, Keelin leaned over and picked the book up. She gently eased the book open and cautiously touched the pages only along the edges. A small envelope slipped into her lap. Different than the first envelope with the cryptic "it is time" message, this envelope was unmarked. It was softly padded and held the same wax seal she had seen earlier. Keelin examined the seal more closely and thought that she was able to discern what looked like an old-fashioned anchor. She laughed softly as she thought about being a descendent of a famous pirate queen. With a little smile, Keelin peeled the seal back and found a stack of euros along with an address for Grace's Cove.

"Well, someone doesn't like to mince words." Keelin was amused at the direct route. She grabbed her iPad and googled the address, pulling up the image function on the map. A thatched cottage met her eyes, perched high on a hill. As she rotated the image, Keelin gasped. The view from the cottage overlooked stunning cliffs and the curve of a cove. In any other city, this would be prime real estate.

Keelin put her iPad down and returned to the book. Picking up the wad of euros, she quickly counted the money. It was more than enough for travel and some odds and ends.

"Well, let's see what this book is all about. I'm not about to get into any dark-magick stuff." One thing Keelin was certain of was that her life could use less drama.

Keelin carefully paged through the book. Hundreds of handwritten spells or poems covered the pages. Unfortunately much of the writing was in Gaelic and completely undecipherable to Keelin. As she paged through she noticed small sheets tucked behind each page. She opened them and found English translations of the Gaelic words. It was evident that someone had labored with this book. This was more than a gift. It was an offering.

Keelin began to examine the weathered handwriting that scrawled across the pages. It was almost as if they were recipes. Yet not. As she read through the ingredients, Keelin realized that most of these were not something you would eat. They were topical ointments and potions used for various ailments. There were even directions for cultivating certain plants under the light of the moon. Spooky, Keelin thought. Yet, for some reason she wasn't scared. Keelin paged through the whole book and found nothing in relation to the devil or dark arts aside from some sort of ritual for protection. From what she could see, this was a healer's book.

Her curiosity piqued, Keelin pulled out her iPad again. She researched "Celtic healer." As Keelin scrolled through the pages of information, she focused on a few key facts.

The Celtic healing tradition is one of the oldest paths and can deepen the connection to the divine energy, ancestors, and the endless renewal of the natural world. Healing enhances the physical body of the person receiving the energy and can resolve pains or injuries of the physical body.

The Celts were a rural people by choice, preferring to live close to nature because of their love of the land and their view of themselves as being the caretakers of Mother

Earth. The Druids were the spiritual guardians of the Celts and made sure that each Celtic citizen led a healthy holistic lifestyle.

It is common to Irish tradition that families of healers are descended from someone who has been given access to healing knowledge. In Ireland families of healers were often said to have obtained their knowledge from ancient books. Great legends and deep superstitions surround these infamous healing books.

With healing comes a word of caution. The seeking of wisdom, including the wisdom of healing, is a dangerous business; death may ensue if healing is used improperly.

Keelin shivered and rubbed her hands up and down her arms. It appeared that there was a long and rich history of healers in Ireland. She wondered how certain people were touched with the gift while others weren't. There had to be more than just Grace O'Malley's bloodline. Was she really a healer? Was this her path? Her stomach took a small nosedive while at the same time her heart seemed to leap and sing. She shook her head. Before making any rash decisions, she needed to do more research. She padded into the kitchen and pulled out a packet of instant chicken soup. Pouring it into a cup, Keelin shook her head as she put the soup into the microwave. Some healer she was. She couldn't even make soup on the stove. How was she to mix complex ointments and heal someone?

Blowing on her soup, Keelin padded back into the living room and curled up with a blanket on the couch. Her mind was spinning with the possibilities and yet her science mind scoffed at this "energy healing" concept. She needed to learn more about Grace O'Malley as well as the Chalice of Ardagh.

Quickly caught up in the rich history of Ireland, Keelin blinked hours later as her iPad battery died. She shook her head and stretched out her legs and arms. Sometimes she had a habit of becoming so engrossed in her research that the hours would slip by unnoticed. She thought about what she had learned. It appeared that Grace O'Malley was the original gangster. Not only did this woman marry twice, birth a child at sea, and murder hundreds of invaders who sought to take her lands, but she also forced political change for her country. Very little was mentioned about her healing powers, though many noted that she had an uncanny ability for anticipating potential threats and circumventing them. It was said that she disappeared when the end of her life came to a close and was never accounted for again. Keelin wondered what had happened to her.

The Chalice of Ardagh also had an interesting history. Though many details were given to the ornamentation and design of this intricate chalice, virtually nothing was known of its true roots. Keelin noted that many of the decorations on the chalice were of animals. It seemed to tie in nicely with the Celtic history of animism. Keelin wondered if a companion piece to the chalice was buried deep in Grace's Cove. The longer she thought about it the more she itched to grab her dive gear and spend the summer treasure hunting.

Keelin stared into space as thoughts raced through her mind. Was she a healer? What were these visions she had? Should she go to Ireland?

Exhausted, her eyes drooped and she fell into a deep sleep on the sofa. A man stepped into her dreams. With dark, unruly hair and blindingly blue eyes, he stared at her through the flames of a bonfire that shot up around them. His eyes seemed to glow in the darkness. Dark water rose up and covered her as she swam towards a glint of gold. Helpless, she couldn't reach it and was swept away only to awake bathed in a cold sweat. Her heart hammered against her chest and she wiped her sweat-soaked hair from her face.

Keelin forced herself to take deep breaths and to calm the hammering of her heart. It was just a dream. It had been a weird day, she reminded herself. The book caught her eye. It was open where it had once been closed. She leaned over to look at the page that it had fallen open to. Written on it was a mixture of herbs to nurture true love.

"Cute. Real cute," she said.

With a sigh, Keelin reached for the phone. It was time to convince her professor that her thesis subject matter could be found on the Emerald Isle.

Chapter Five

THE PLANE TOUCHED down with a little bounce that rattled the cabin. Keelin clenched her armrest and continued to say a "Hail Mary." She loved to travel but she very specifically hated when planes landed. Not the take-off and not the flight – but always the landing. As the smaller plane that she had taken from Dublin to Shannon taxied to a stop, Keelin exhaled a long breath before she gathered her purse and backpack. She thought about all that had transpired in the last few weeks. She was unsure if she was about to meet her destiny or if she was chasing a foolish superstition. It had taken some convincing on her part, but with enough research and the fact that her professor was half-Irish, her school had agreed to a summer in Ireland and a topic change of her thesis. She could only hope that the dark waters of the cove would provide enough information for her to write a thesis. Her mother had been more difficult to convince. While she had been initially supportive, when Keelin had made the decision to go, Margaret had lost it.

Keelin reviewed the difficult scene in her head. Margaret had stubbornly offered to pay for the rest of Keelin's graduate school as well as her rent for the next five years if she didn't go to Ireland. With a promise of twice-weekly phone calls and many emails, her mother had finally agreed to her decision. Keelin shuddered a bit as she thought about Margaret's tears. She had rarely seen her mother cry. Keelin thought that some of the emotion had to come from the passing of Margaret's mother. Although, Margaret hadn't flown out for the funeral or mentioned anything of the sort, Keelin thought now. She wondered if much of Margaret's emotion came from her being scared of being alone in Boston, or of what secrets of Margaret's Keelin might find when she arrived in Ireland.

"Are you alright there?" A lilting voice startled Keelin from her thoughts. A young woman waited for her in the aisle. Tiny in stature, with dark curling hair and greenish-yellow eyes, she smiled kindly at Keelin.

"Oh, yes, I'm sorry." Keelin stood up and immediately felt like a giant. She towered over this slip of a girl. Keelin mentally kicked herself. At 5'9" and with generous hips, she knew that she was a larger girl, but she always had to work at not feeling like a giant when she was around tiny women.

"Not a problem. Looks like you were daydreaming a wee bit." The girl snagged a huge bag one-handed from the overhead bin and swung it over her shoulder. "American, I see. Here for a holiday?"

"No, I am going to Grace's Cove for the summer to write my thesis."

"No kidding. I thought you looked familiar. You must be an O'Brien. I can tell by the eyes." The girl stared into Keelin's distinct brandy-toned eyes. "That would make us cousins of sorts. I'm Caitriona."

At Keelin's blank stare, she laughed. "That's Irish for Katherine. Call me Cait."

"Hi, Cait. I'm Keelin O'Brien. And, how are we cousins? Do you live in Grace's Cove?" Keelin asked as they walked towards baggage claim together.

"Yes, ma'am, I certainly do. I own Gallagher's Pub. It's the best stop for a pint and live music in town. Or so I say." Cait laughed up at Keelin with her dancing eyes. "I know all the gossip in town. So if you have any questions about anything, stop in and see me. You should stop in anyway and get accustomed to village life. You'll do well to have a few friends on your side." With those enigmatic words, Cait strode away to pick up her bag.

"Wait. Why wouldn't I have friends?" Keelin hurried to keep up with her. Cait moved fast.

Cait stopped and turned. Shock was apparent on her face. "Why, because of your family reputation for being witches. Have you heard about your grandmother? A lovely lady, but I made sure never to cross her."

"Oh, stop. Do witches even exist? I heard that my grandma was a bit off and a good healer – but a witch? No."

"Hey, listen. Fiona half-raised me. I never saw anything that indicated she was a witch. That being said – her healing abilities are famous. Perhaps a touch of the fae. I simply stayed on her good side and I had no problems. Don't worry, most of the people in town are nice and you shouldn't run into too many problems. I've got to run. Come see me for a pint. I'm serious. I could use some girl time and would love to hear about America."

With that, Cait strolled off and hefted two huge duffle bags as if they were nothing.

"Witches. Lovely." Keelin blew off the Irish mysticism and collected her luggage. She had forgotten to ask Cait about where her grandmother was buried. She wondered if the village had turned out for the funeral or not.

Keelin pulled out a folded piece of paper with printed instructions and headed for the remote lot. Keelin prayed that she hadn't been taken for a ride and that the car that she had purchased prior to the trip was in its spot. As she approached what could loosely be called a truck, she groaned. This rust bucket looked as if it would fall apart the first time she shifted into third gear. A dull red, with paint peeling and rust creeping up the frame, the car looked like it would run on a wing and a prayer. Keelin felt under the front bumper for the key in the magnet box and climbed onto the front seat.

She stared at the empty dashboard and looked to her right at the steering wheel.

"Duh." Sliding across the front bench seat, Keelin hoped that nobody had noticed her mistake.

"Steering wheel on the right, drive on the left," she muttered to herself as she turned the key and prayed as the truck shuddered to life.

"There we go, girl. You got this. Come on, baby." Sweet-talking the truck, Keelin eased out into traffic and began the drive to Grace's Cove.

After several near mishaps, and cheerful waves to the cars she almost hit, Keelin felt like she was getting in the groove of driving on the left side of the road. Irish roads were notorious for their narrow passes, twisty curves, and precarious blind spots. The route to Grace's Cove boasted all of these. Keelin decided to go slow and soak it in. Well, her truck made the decision for her as anything over 45 miles per hour (kilometers! she thought to herself) made the truck rattle dangerously. Keelin hoped that it would hold together long enough for her to make it to the village.

Several almost misses later, Keelin shuddered the truck over a large hill and gasped. The village spread out before her, quaintly perched at the base of the cliffs, overlooking the ocean. If she were to send a postcard of Ireland, it would bear this picture. Rolling green hills met harsher ridges and tapered down into the colorful cottages that clustered around the curved harbor. A sense of home rose within her and she smiled. This just looked like a place where everyone would be happy. Looking forward to her first pot of tea and scones with real cream on the side, Keelin made her way to the parking spots that lined the harbor. She shut the car off and breathed a sigh of relief. The rust bucket had held up surprisingly well.

Smiling, Keelin hefted a backpack over her shoulder and looked around for a grocer. She had no idea what sort of supplies were left after her grandmother had passed and was reluctant to be stuck in the hills with no food and un-reliable transportation. Keelin stopped and breathed deep-ly. There was something about the scent of ocean air that made her blood sing. She always knew when she was close to water. Keelin watched several fishermen pull their boats in and unload the day's catch. They would go back out again before sunset. Tiny, colorful boats bobbed further out on the water, and gulls swooped around the fisher-men's boats. The sun was shining, a slight breeze tickled her neck, and Keelin fought to keep a smile off her face. This was going to be the best summer ever. Except for that witches thing Cait had mentioned. She'd have to look into that.

Keelin headed towards the middle of the village and looked for a grocer. Shops clustered together and hugged the narrow, curved road that wandered up a hill into the village. Keelin admired all of the vibrant colors used on the storefronts and wished that America didn't always make their shops so steely and gray. There was something that just worked with the mishmash of colors and building ma-terials that made up these little shops. Keelin stopped to admire some lacework in a weaver's shop. Two women walked out and the older one stopped and gasped, staring right at her. She grabbed her companion's arm, pointed, and hustled across the street.

I wonder what that was all about? Keelin thought. The village certainly had a large amount of B&Bs; people shouldn't have reacted to a tourist like that. Keelin continued up the hill past a weathered old man. He stared at her eyes and spit at her – making the sign of the cross.

What was going on here? Her idyllic picture of a perfect summer vacation was beginning to unravel if this was the way that people in the village acted.

Keelin found the grocer tucked around the corner and wandered the aisles. How was she going to cook? She didn't even know if this hut had a microwave. Maybe it would be best if she just went with the basics, as she had no idea what she was walking into. In fact, what if there was no refrigerator? She laughed at herself. Of course there was. She hoped so. Keelin gingerly put the deli meat back and headed for non-refrigerator type food. She stocked up on bread, apples, peanut butter & jelly and some almonds. It was enough food for a little while and she would be sure to come back to town for more once she got the lay of the land.

Keelin approached the middle-aged woman with a hairnet at the checkout line. The woman sized her up and said, "You must be Fiona O'Brien's granddaughter. I can see it in your eyes. We've always wondered when Margaret would let you come back."

"Oh, do you know my mother?" Keelin asked. Finally, a friend.

"Aye, I did at that. We used to work together. She should have stayed here to see if it would work out with Sean, though I guess that I understood her need to go. I'm assuming you are heading up to the cottage? You'll need to get on the road then before dark or you'll never find it."

"Um, okay. What is your name? Can you tell me more about why people are being weird to me?" Keelin asked in a rush of breath. She needed to know what she was walking into.

"The name is Sarah Gallagher. We're related in an odd sort of way. As I'm sure you know, your family doesn't have the best reputation in town. Yet, at the same time, you have the best reputation that you can have. You'll have to sort this out for yourself." Sarah quickly finished her bagging and dismissed Keelin to help her next customer.

Keelin felt out of sorts and fairly nervous. What was she doing walking into a situation like this? And nobody would give her answers. She trudged down the hill to her car, ignoring the curious looks cast her way. She would just figure this out for herself then. Keelin tossed her bags in the bed of the truck and got in the passenger side of the truck, slammed her hand on the dashboard in annoyance, and scooted over to the driver's side. She would get the hang of this, she swore to herself.

Turning the key in the ignition, she prayed. "Come on, baby, we've got a ways to go. Let's do this. Come on." The car chugged and rattled but the engine never caught.

"Damn it. You have got to be kidding me." Frustrated, Keelin opened the door and went around to the hood. Unable to locate the latch to open the hood, she slammed her fist on the top and let loose with a few of her more colorful curses.

Laughter interrupted her tantrum. "Need help, miss?" A lilting Irish brogue with a deep tenor broke through her tirade. Keelin turned to meet the owner of the voice, grateful for someone who would be nice to her.

The sun blinded her momentarily and all Keelin could see were piercing blue eyes. The deep blue of the ocean in the cove, these were the eyes in her dream. A shiver ran through her and she went a little lightheaded. Stumbling, Keelin grasped the rusted edge of the hood for support. As the man moved towards her, she made out the rest of him and drew in a deep breath. She was in trouble if all of the men in Ireland looked like this. Dark curly hair framed a chiseled face that Armani would have paid millions for to advertise their clothes in their catalog. Broad shoulders tapered to slim hips, and he walked with the ease of a man confident both on land and at sea. A day's growth of beard marred his tanned skin, and his thick lips drew into a tight line as he saw her face. His smile disappeared and he stopped, his confidence gone. Annoyance crossed his face and he cursed. Keelin got the distinct impression that he would have walked away had he not already spoken to her. Duty bound, he moved forward.

"Yes, thank you. My car won't start and I don't know how to open the hood. Or what is under the hood for that matter." Keelin smiled, hoping to wipe the annoyance from his face.

He stopped close to her. With one long gaze he took her in from head to toe and dismissed her as he turned to the truck and popped the hood.

"Excuse me, what is your name?" Keelin was miffed. She'd had her fill of rude strangers for the day.

"Flynn." He fiddled with some wires and went around to her driver's side. The car roared to life.

"Well, doesn't that just figure?" Even more unexplainably pissed, Keelin huffed out a breath.

"Well, Mr. Flynn, I kindly thank you for taking such time out of your day to help the likes of me. Could you spare a moment and tell me what was actually wrong with my car? If it isn't too much for you, sir?" Keelin could be sarcastic with the best of them.

"Loose ground wire was giving you an intermittent connection when you were trying to start it. I've tightened it. No charge." Flynn stared at her one more time and turned to go.

"Wait! Don't you want to know my name?" Keelin surprised herself and grabbed his hand. A surge of power slapped between their palms, heating her immediately, and her skin tingled. Sensations whiplashed through her and pooled low in her stomach. Shocked, Keelin stared into Flynn's angry face.

"I know exactly who you are, Keelin O'Brien." Flynn stomped off and whistled sharply. A dog that Keelin had not seen before ran from her perch on the boardwalk and walked by his side, turning its head to stare at her.

"Well, thanks! Thanks a lot! I'll be sure to write home about the amazing Irish hospitality!" Keelin yelled after him. Flynn lifted his hand in a "go away" gesture.

Chapter Six

$\mathbf{F}$LYNN'S HEART POUNDED in his chest as he whistled for Teagan and walked away from Keelin. Of course, he knew who she was. Over the past year, her image had haunted his dreams.

He let out a small sigh as he walked up the pier towards where his fishing boat was docked. Untying the line from the pier, he waited for Teagan to hop into the boat before he leapt away from the dock. Motoring slowly from the harbor, Flynn worked to bring his pulse under control.

Lush curves, molten brown eyes, and hair that he ached to see spread over his pillows flashed through his mind. Keelin was his fantasy girl. She'd stepped into his dreams little over a year ago and Flynn had had a hard time not measuring every woman he had met since then to her.

To her. Some figment of his imagination. Until he'd caught a glance of a photo in Fiona's cottage and realized that his fantasy woman was none other than Fiona's estranged granddaughter, Keelin. Confusion had laced through him as he had stared down at the picture. Keelin, full of life and youth, laughed up at the camera from the grass that she sat on. She couldn't have been more than fourteen and her beauty only hinted at the woman she was to become. It had been like a punch to the gut when Flynn had realized that his dream girl was real.

Seeing her today, angry at her truck, Flynn had literally felt the world shift out from under him. How had he dreamed about her? How had he known?

His response to her in person was as visceral as in his dreams. He groaned as lust pooled low in his stomach and he ached to wrap Keelin in his arms. Yet, the fact that she had shown up in his dreams made him distrustful. How was it possible that he had known of her…her scent, her smile, her very essence…before ever meeting her?

What he didn't understand typically made him angry. Flynn liked a measure of control in his life. There was something about Keelin that made him want to throw caution to the wind and dive right in for a taste.

Scared that he was already too far gone, Flynn found himself gunning the engine and tearing out into the ocean. Away from the promise that Keelin hinted at.

Chapter Seven

"WHAT THE HELL WAS THAT?" Keelin thought. She was pissed. One surly Irishman had heated her blood more quickly than the last five Boston elites that her mom had set her up with. She chalked it up to a long dry spell in her love life and studied the directions on her paper. A flush crept up her cheeks. Damn that man for making her angry and hot in the same moment. She hadn't been this disturbed in a while.

Muttering under her breath, she pulled out into the street and almost hit a car in the right lane.

"Damn it!" Keelin whipped the wheel to the left and moved over. She made a note to calm down before driving here. She was bound to get herself hurt. Her truck chugged up the hill and onto a narrow road that wound deeper into the hills. Bushes and rocks concealed corners and most turns were blind. Keelin took deep breaths and drove slowly. Even so, she only narrowly missed the weathered sign. O'Brien's Road was etched on a small piece of wood, the red of the paint almost worn off.

"Here we go." Gravel coated the road and the truck shuddered as it worked itself over the bumps and grooves that furrowed the track up the hill. Keelin wound the truck higher up the hill, passing by worn fences and pastures dotted with spray-painted sheep. Why in the world were the sheep hot pink? Keelin made a note to ask someone about that.

Punk-rock sheep, she laughed to herself. Her friends back home in the Boston music scene would find that funny. She turned a blind corner and let out a shriek. A herd of sheep blocked her path and didn't appear to be in the mood to move.

Keelin laid on the horn. Nothing. They stared back at her balefully, and stood their ground.

She rolled down her window. "Hey. You. Get! Get out of here." Frustrated and figuring she had been tested enough, she moved the truck forward. The sheep bolted quickly and Keelin laughed. Now she was beginning to feel a little more like an Irishwoman.

Keelin turned another corner and her world opened up.

"Oh. Oh God. Oh, I just can't." Her voice caught in her throat and unexpected tears pricked at her eyes. The sheer beauty of the landscape before her was unapologetic in its magnificence. The stone hut was nestled by two rocky outcroppings to block the wind. Below the hut, the hills stretched wide before kissing the sea. The stunning green hills rolled down to arrogant cliffs that jutted into an almost perfect half-circle of a cove. Grace's Cove. A small sand beach lay in the dead center of the cover and a narrow path wound through the cliffs to the beach. The sun was blinding in its brilliance, diamonds of light shattered across the surface of the water and the green of the grass was a perfect contrast to the blue of the water that mirrored the same hue in the sky. Keelin felt like she was on top of the world.

I would never leave here if I didn't have to, she thought. As she turned to look around she began to make out the intricacies in the landscape. Various paths wandered in different directions over the hills, and stone markers were set at odd points throughout the land.

Was that a stone circle? Her eyes strained to make out what appeared to be a series of rocks set in a circle. The plant life was lush and there were various ribbons tied on bushes and flowers. A high brick wall segmented an area past the outcropping, and vines coated it. Keelin wondered what was past the wall.

So this is to be my home for a while? I can live with this. Keelin looked forward to an adventure for the summer, and where else could she get it but in this slice of heaven? Keelin put her backpack on and hefted her grocery sacks from the back of the truck. Turning, she looked at the mountains at her back. They rose behind her and sheltered the house, the land, and the cove. Keelin squinted. For a second she thought she saw a man and a dog high up on the ridge overlooking the house. Shaking her head, she looked again and the ridge was empty.

Keelin walked towards the hut. It was really quite a bit larger than a hut but Keelin liked the romantic thought of staying in a hut on the water's edge all summer. She would be sure to call it a hut to her friends back home. It was more of a wide square house that had two larger rooms jutting from the back. Built of round gray stones and dark wood beams, the house looked as if it was a part of the landscape. It was as if it was built for this land and this land alone.

Keelin wasn't sure if she should knock or not. It was just her here, right? She pulled the latch and went in. Light filtered through the single-paned windows, dust motes causing the light to shoot like beams across the worn farm table that stood in the middle of the room. The door opened directly into the main room, the hub of the house. One side was a small kitchen, with a wood-burning stove and a pantry. Two doors led off the back of the room and into what she presumed were bedrooms. The predominant focus of the room was the large table in the middle, which was riddled with jars, flowers, twine, and bowls. Keelin moved towards the table and noticed the walls were lined with shelves. Bottles upon bottles were stacked neatly on the shelves, and small labels were attached to them all. Keelin walked over to a shelf and saw powders of all sorts and colors. They looked like spices, but Keelin wouldn't be doing any taste tests anytime soon.

"So, you've finally arrived, then."

Keelin let out a screech and dropped her bags to the floor.

A chuckle came out of a dim corner to Keelin's right. She had missed this alcove when she had first walked in. A woman sat in a wooden rocker, the arms and back of the chair seemingly carved from a single piece of wood. Keelin wanted to sit in that chair. It hugged the woman in it and they rocked as if they were one. Keelin's own eyes peered at her from under an impressive head of long, curly gray hair. Her hair leaped and roped around her head, tied in areas with twine, with small flowers placed behind her ears.

Easily eighty years old, when Fiona smiled the years dropped from her face. She reminded Keelin of the hippies that often staged protests in the Boston Common. An earthiness clung to the old woman, yet a stillness and gentleness radiated from her. Her hands stuck out from a blue wool cape and were deftly tying twine around bunches of dried herbs. Paper labels were lined up neatly next to the bundles. The smell of lavender teased Keelin's nose and soothed her at the same time.

"Grandma?" It was a statement more than a question. There was no other person this woman could be.

"Well, yes, of course, Keelin. Who did you think it would be?" Fiona laughed up at Keelin and rose to embrace her. Another tiny woman, Keelin leaned over to embrace her awkwardly. She could feel her thin bones beneath the cape and instantly worried for her health.

"I'm just fine, Keelin. And call me Fiona," Fiona said with a smile. "Come, come. Let me feed you." Fiona bustled over to the small stove, where a pot was simmering. "I made extra for you today." She pulled brown bread from the ledge of the window, where it had been cooling in the open air, wrapped in a checkered kitchen towel.

"I'm sorry, but I thought you were, um, well, dead," Keelin stammered out.

"I know you did. Silly child, listening to your mother. Margaret certainly should have known that I was the only one who would send you that book. Ah, she always did like to make things difficult," Fiona said as she carefully measured a creamy chowder into brown stoneware bowls. Moving to the table, she placed the bowls on brightly colored mats, and brought the bread over with a dish of butter.

"Sit, sit. It's so nice to have company." Fiona happily chattered on and asked Keelin about her flight. "You're such a beauty, as I expected. You have the O'Brien coloring and stature – that strawberry-blonde hair, the brandy-colored eyes, and that body. You'll make a man very lucky someday."

Keelin stared at Fiona with her mouth open. She'd never been described in quite that way before. Her hair and eyes often received compliments. But her size-twelve frame and generous hips and bosom were not often complimented in the land of WASPs and stick-straight blondes that populated Boston.

"Um, thank you. Really. I'm sorry. Thank you and I'm not trying to be rude, but don't you think this was all a really dramatic way to get me to come here?" Keelin didn't like being surprised and was already on edge from a long day of travel. Having her grandmother for her summer roommate had not been in her plans.

Fiona sighed. "Well, you know the Irish are prone to a bit of drama, my dear. But, yes, I sincerely thought this was the best way to bring you here. It is time, after all."

"Okay, enough with this 'it is time' stuff. Time for what?" Keelin refused to sit. She felt like she was a part of some conspiracy and everyone was in on it but her.

"Well, time for you to claim your birthright, my dear. Now. Eat. There is plenty of time for talk. You need your sleep and your rest before we start your lessons first thing in the morning," Fiona said as she blew on her soup spoon.

"Lessons? I have a thesis to write, you know," Keelin said as she sat.

"Yes, dear. You'll have time for all that. Now, tell me about your mother." Fiona looked sweet, but she could certainly evade questions with the best of them. So this was where her mother had gotten it from, Keelin thought.

"Well, I'm glad you aren't dead," Keelin said, and sat down. The bowl of soup called to her and her stomach grumbled in response. Her first bite of the thick brown bread had her taste buds humming. They just didn't make bread like this in the States.

Fiona laughed. "Yes, me as well. Now, tell me about Boston."

Keelin filled Fiona in on her life in Boston while she devoured two bowls of soup. She was famished. After dinner, Fiona started a small fire in the wood-burning stove and showed her to a small room at the back of the house.

"It isn't much, but should suit you just fine," Fiona said as she smoothed a brightly patched coverlet over pure white Irish linen sheets. The small bed was tucked beneath an alcove that offered a large window that overlooked the cove. A window across the room looked up to the mountain ridge above. A threadbare hooked rug covered the worn floorboards and a small table with a stoneware water pitcher stood in the corner. The simplicity of the room contrasted with the striking views and made it what it should be – a room solely about the world outside.

"This is beautiful, thank you." Keelin felt a rush of knowing. This was her room.

"Aye, yes, this is yours." Fiona looked at her. She knew. She moved towards the door. "Sleep, my dear. Sleep. There is much to learn."

Keelin put her bags on the floor and watched the last traces of light hug the water before the sun dipped off the edge. It felt like she had stepped into another lifetime. She quickly stripped, used the small attached bathroom, and put on a short tank and boy shorts to sleep in. The linen sheets were cool and smooth. They enveloped her, and the exhaustion of the day caught up with her. Keelin quickly drifted into a dreamless sleep.

She woke to dead quiet and confusion. Where was she? Disorientated, Keelin shot up and fumbled for her phone. She clicked it on and her eyes adjusted in the dim light.

3:00 a.m. Her time was all messed up. As her eyes adjusted to the room, she saw the bright moonlight shining through the window. Intrigued, she rose to her knees and leaned to look out over Grace's Cove. The stark cliffs highlighted the perfect half-circle of the cove. The ocean glowed to the horizon, reflecting the soft white light of the moon. Keelin loved nights like this. She had always dreamed of sailing in the path of the moon to lands undiscovered. Her eyes traced the light of the moon that trailed across the water and she gasped as she realized that the light stopped once it hit the cove. She stretched up and leaned forward more. That couldn't be right. It had to be a trick of the light or the angle of the house. The waters of the cove were dark. No reflection. How could that be? Keelin quietly lifted the glass window and leaned as far out as she could, her long hair tangled over her shoulders. The cove remained dark. A movement caught her eye. A dark animal raced across the field away from the cove. Was that a wolf? Did Ireland even have wolves? Keelin tried to pull herself back in quickly and caught her hair on the windowsill.

Damn it. She was always doing klutzy stuff like this. As she reached to untangle her hair, her eyes tracked the animal approaching her. With some trepidation, she worked quickly at the knot in the hair. Gasping, she glanced up as the wolf drew near and she realized a man was walking behind it. She had seen that walk before. Flynn walked with the ease of a man confident in his body...in his right to be on this land. She could swear that she saw the blue of his eyes glinting. Keelin looked down and realized the picture she made: her breasts were all but falling out of her thin tank top and she had no bra on. She looked up and his eyes seemed to bore into hers. A small hum pooled deep in her stomach. Her nipples tightened.

Furious, she ripped her hair from the sill and sat back, slamming the window. She could have sworn she heard his laughter. What was Flynn doing out on their land at 3:00 a.m.? And why was the cove dark? Keelin's science mind couldn't come up with any explanation other than that the house was situated at an odd angle. Frustrated, and sexually aware, Keelin went back to sleep with thoughts of bright-eyed men and strange dogs drifting through her head.

Chapter Eight

THE SMELL OF BACON and the growling of her stomach teased Keelin awake. What better way to wake up? Squinting, she saw that the light was mellow and the morning was young. She pulled on an old sweatshirt and her cottage socks and padded into the kitchen.

"Good morning, sleeping beauty. Did you rest well?" Fiona asked from the stove.

"Yes, Keelin, how did you sleep?" A deep male voice startled Keelin into brushing her hair out of her face. Flynn sat comfortably at the kitchen table, finishing a full Irish and drinking a pot of tea. His blue eyes glinted at her. Uncomfortable, Keelin crossed her arms in front of her chest and wished she had put on pajama pants. Her boy shorts barely covered her. She tried to surreptitiously tug her sweatshirt down while keeping her arm crossed over her chest.

Flynn watched her in amusement. She curled her upper lip at him. What was it about this man that made her want to swat at him?

"Breakfast, my dear?" Fiona smiled at her, a quiet joy radiating from her. She had a full kitchen and was happy as could be.

"Just tea, please." Keelin wasn't sure if she could bring herself to sit down to breakfast with Flynn. As if reading her mind, he smiled and got up, taking his dishes to the sink.

"Lovely as always, Fiona. Thanks for breakfast. Let me know if you need any other leaks patched up." Flynn kissed her grandmother gently and nodded to Keelin before leaving.

"Ugh, that man," Keelin huffed out, and grabbed a piece of bacon.

"Gorgeous, isn't he?" Fiona smiled and hummed as she cleaned up.

"Well, yeah, but he's kind of a jerk too."

"The best ones always are, honey."

"What's his story, anyway?" Keelin asked, trying to act casual.

"Flynn? Ahh, he has quite the story, which I imagine he will tell you in his own time. He's a local fisherman, owns the land bordering ours, and acts as an overall handyman for things that I can't handle on my own. He certainly has been a blessing to me. Surly, though. A good woman could change that." Fiona dimpled up at Keelin.

"I don't think so. That man is trouble. Who walks the lands at 3:00 a.m.? I don't trust him."

"Well, this is as much his land as it is ours. It was a lovely night for a walk last night, what with that full moon," Fiona said.

"Still. It's weird," Keelin huffed into her mug of tea.

"Why don't you get changed? I have some plans for us this morning." Fiona said enigmatically.

Keelin took her tea with her to the shower. As she combed through her long hair she couldn't help flashing back to the dreams that racked her after she had seen Flynn the night before. Sweaty skin, arms entwined, and the flames of a fire. It had all been so pagan – so earthy. It was enough to make her blush as she showered and tried to remove the images from her head. She refused to give Flynn more headspace. More importantly, it was time to grill her grandmother about the book and the mysterious dark cove.

With a nod to the sunny day, Keelin put on cargo walking shorts, a simple tank, and brought out her Wellingtons. She wanted to get a better look at the land.

"Feeling better, dear?" Fiona had changed and had her own hiking boots on as well as a faded leather satchel that she wore across her body. Soft butter-yellow gloves were tucked in her pocket along with shears.

"Yes, thank you. I want to ask you about the book that you sent me. And I have questions about the cove too."

"Yes, yes, of course. Your time for lessons must start. Come along." Fiona handed Keelin a matching bag, outfitted with gloves and sheers as well. Keelin opened the bag to find a stack of cotton bags and twine. A small notepad and pencil were tucked in a pocket. She briefly debated bringing her phone and camera but realized that they wouldn't be needed.

"Have you heard tales of healers? Wise women?" Fiona interrupted her thoughts as they left the cottage.

"Yes, I looked it up a bit after I spoke with my mother about the book. I can't decide if it is witchcraft or something different. It all seems to blend in and out and weave around."

"Perfect! That is a wonderful description. It *is* all woven in and out together. The universal power. There is magick, you know." Fiona peered over at Keelin.

"Yeah, I mean, I guess." Keelin was going to reserve judgment on that one.

"Well, you'll hear rumors of witchcraft, and people in town love to gossip. But they speak of things that they know nothing of. I'd love to be a witch. It sounds like it would be a lot of fun. Alas, I am not. I don't cast spells. That doesn't mean that I am without power, my dear. Nor are you. If you are willing to truly claim your birthright, then I may teach you."

Keelin stared at Fiona as they approached a rock formation. Piles of mismatched rocks stood in a circle around a patch of dirt. The green hills rolled below them and the waters of the cove were gentle.

"I guess that I don't really know what you mean," Keelin said hesitantly.

"Don't you?" Fiona looked at her. Her small frame seemed to grow in stature as she stared into Keelin's eyes.

"I, uh, well. I've had some moments. Just things that happen. I don't really have an explanation for them. So, I just ignore it. Is that what you are talking about?" Keelin was nervous. Her skin was tingling. She could feel sweat pooling on her lower back under her tank top. She never talked about this. Keelin had built her protective walls at a young age and now she felt like she was being stripped bare.

Fiona held out her arm. She reached into her bag and grabbed her shears, quickly slashing a shallow cut across the top of her arm. Keelin gasped. "Grandma! Don't do that. Why?" Without thinking, Keelin covered the wound with her hand and applied pressure. She felt a quick sting on her own arm and knew it was fine. She removed her hand as Fiona smiled at her and looked down at her arm, now unmarked. A faint bruise had appeared on Keelin's arm in the same spot that Fiona had sliced her own.

Keelin's head was hammering. It always happened this way. She moved too fast. She didn't think. What would her grandmother think of her? People always freaked when this happened. This was one of the reasons she rarely had long relationships. Most men couldn't handle or under-stand what she was. She didn't even know what she was.

Fiona smiled at her and gently laid her hand on Keelin's bruise. The pain lessened and her headache disap-peared. Keelin looked down to see that the bruise had fad-ed away.

"You're a healer, my dear. A natural. And it's time you learned how to harness and manage your power or you will cause yourself great damage."

"A healer? For real? I thought that was all an old wives' tale." Keelin felt foolish as she said it. How could it be old wives' tales when she had just seen it with her own eyes? How long could she refuse to acknowledge what she was?

Fiona ushered her into the circle. "As you know, with any power comes responsibility. There are rules to be learned. Lessons to begin. Medicines and natural earthly remedies can enhance your healing. The universe has a great and resourceful power which you must harness. The Celtic history of healing is a rich and powerful one. We respect nature, animals, and the universal energy. Celtic healers have long believed in the power of natural remedies combined with harnessing the universal energy available to all of us. Some of us are more inclined to this gift than others." Fiona nodded at her and pulled out several small bags of herbs.

"There are, however, dark energies that can harm you. This is why you must learn simple ways to protect yourself. When learning, I ask that you work within a circle of protection. We issue our prayers here and we set our intention to use our powers for the highest purpose of helping others. We are healers. We have a responsibility to others, and to ourselves. Sometimes, with this gift comes the ability to see certain things. There will be times where you get flashes of what will come. Or you can catch a thought of someone else's. These are natural intuitive abilities that we all have – yet they are slightly tweaked for us. This is a legacy to us from Grace O'Malley."

Keelin couldn't even deny what her grandmother said. When a soul meets its own truth for the first time there are no walls that can be put up. No shields. This resonated in her as purely and deeply as the air she breathed.

"My mother?" Keelin asked.

"Your mother, God bless her, has her own powers. She is not a healer and was often embarrassed or scared by that which she refused to learn. Your mother is empathic and has a strong ability to read people's feelings and decisions. It is what makes her an excellent real estate agent yet not a good healer. If she absorbed all of the emotions of those who were sick she would literally crumble upon herself. She learned to shield her emotions at a young age, but this world scared her and she fled to protect you. What she refused to see until you were old enough was that you can't flee from what you are. I could no more stop you from healing than you could stop her from dyeing her hair blonde."

Keelin smiled. It was true. Her mom went into New York City every month for the perfect Fifth Avenue blonde. She claimed that Boston hair stylists couldn't even get it right.

"I, I've always done this. I didn't know why. It scared the shit out of me. I remember when I was young and a car hit our cat. I was so distraught that I picked him up and ran with him to our house. I could feel his pain; his two back legs were broken and I was certain the vet would put him down. I held him and wished with everything I had that he would be okay. I cried, and cried, and prayed. I covered him with my body and held him and everything went black. I came to and my mom was shaking me awake. Our cat was running in circles around me. I was on the floor and began throwing up. I was sick for two weeks." Keelin hadn't thought about that in a long time. Her mom had refused to speak of it with her until she had brought it up during their recent talk. It had scared her at the time and they had come to a silent agreement to never speak of it.

"Ah, yes. Raw power unchecked. Your love was true and your intentions pure. You were able to heal your beloved cat yet without protecting yourself you took the pain into you. Sickness has to go somewhere. If you don't learn to direct it outward, you will absorb it and it will poison you. Had you done this with someone deathly ill, you very well could have killed yourself." Fiona walked around the circle as she talked, tidying up the center and snipping off leaves from plants that hung into the circle. She tucked a few pieces into her bag and pulled out the book.

"Are you ready for your first lesson?" Fiona asked.

Still adjusting to the shift in her world, Keelin could only nod. This was not how she had expected her summer to turn out.

"All healers must learn to protect themselves. You are a source of light and universal energy that allows you to heal others. However, there will always be dark energies that seek to take your light as well as the fact that you can't heal without directing the pain or sickness somewhere. Without proper protection, you'll kill yourself or allow a dark energy to break through and latch on to you."

"Okay, this is totally creepy. I don't want to get involved in any of this." Keelin stumbled out of the circle. Her breath hitched as she started to walk the path back. Dark energies were too much for her. She felt the long dregs of panic begin to claw at her stomach. Was her grandmother talking about demons? The devil? Heat flashed through her and Keelin broke out in a sweat. She had no frame of reference for handling any of this. Science didn't address demons and Catholicism shunned them.

"You can't ignore what you are, Keelin. You'll die. You must either give away your power or use it."

The words stopped her. Their truth resonated deeply in Keelin. She had a choice to make. Keelin stared at the water and trembled at opening the door to what she had kept locked away for so long. She was scared to lose her tightly knit control over what and who she was.

"You'll be safe, Keelin. But you must learn." Fiona's voice was gentle.

Keelin turned. Her grandmother stood in the circle, her white hair whipping in the breeze. Her weathered hands held bunches of herbs and a leather cord wrapped around a crystal. Destiny came in the strangest of forms, Keelin thought.

"Why do you say that I will die?" Keelin needed to know.

"If you have a child, and your child becomes ill, you will give everything you have to save them. Without proper training and protection you will die in protecting what you love. This goes for your one true love as well. Your purity of love will make your strength of healing the highest it can be and in exchange you will give your life if you remain untrained."

The thought of being a mother slapped at Keelin. She had always rebelled against it. Yet…yet something tugged in her. Deep down. It was hard to argue with the absolute truth behind Fiona's words.

"Okay, I will stay and I will learn protection. But you really scared me with the whole dark energy talk. I'm not into that voodoo, conjuring spirits stuff." Keelin wanted to be firm on this point.

Fiona laughed and gestured for Keelin to join her in the circle.

"Where there is light, there will be dark. You can't change it any more than you can ignore it. All you can do is learn to protect yourself the best that you may. To ignore doing so is unconscionable."

Nodding, Keelin stepped back into the circle.

"Now, first thing's first. Draw a circle, step into a circle, build a circle with small stones, sticks, chalk, twine…anything around you. A circle is an age-old sign for protection and safety. Yes, the witches use the same and it is for good reason. Do not ignore me on this one particular aspect."

Keelin pulled out her notebook and began to take notes.

"Circle, got it. What next?"

Fiona began to rattle off simple prayers for protection.

"You always want to ask your angels and lightbearers for their help and protection. They are here for you."

Keelin nodded diligently and continued to write.

Fiona handed over the leather necklace with a stone attached.

"Wear this when you are doing healing work. It helps to absorb and deflect any negative energy. It will also help you to channel your purest form of energy towards the work you are doing."

The leather cord was knotted and wrapped in an intricate braided pattern and it circled a crystal that was easily the size of her palm. The clarity of the stone belied the strength it held. Keelin admired the craft with which the necklace had been made. The beauty of the design reflected strength and delicacy at the same time.

"Thank you, this is lovely."

"It was Grace O'Malley's."

The enormity of what Fiona said struck her. The crystal warmed in her palm and she was flooded with emotions of hundreds of years past. Flashes of battles at sea, giving birth, and chanting around the cove whipped through Keelin's mind. Her stomach heaved as powerful emotion swamped her. Keelin grabbed Fiona's hand and Fiona steadied her.

"That will happen sometimes when a stone first connects with its new owner. It recognizes your blood."

Keelin was dizzy and her vision blurred for a moment. Slowly, the panic drained from her and she was left with a softly knowing power. Confidence soothed her like a cool balm.

"It's a beautiful feeling, Keelin, yet a responsibility as well. Always tread carefully with your abilities," Fiona warned. "Now that you have learned some basic protection skills and the amulet has recognized you, we can go to the cove."

"Really? I can't wait." Keelin bounced on her toes. The cove held so many unanswered questions. She was itching to get her dive gear and to get a closer look at what lay under its waters.

"Can we go back so I can get some of my equipment?" Keelin asked.

"Not today, Keelin. You need to be accepted by the cove first or you will know its wrath."

"Okay, so, come on now. Mom told me some of the rumors but is it really haunted? Is there treasure? Why can't people go there?" Keelin's inquisitive mind had a whole list of questions for Fiona and she peppered her with them as she tagged along behind Fiona.

Fiona stopped walking and turned to look at Keelin.

"You must always respect the cove. It is from there that your powers come. You are a part of it as much as you are a part of this earth. Haunted, not haunted, treasure or not – you must always respect it. The cove will do as the cove does. You can no more examine it and categorize it than you can predict it. The cove simply is."

"There is no way that I can believe that. There is an explanation for everything," Keelin said as she stared into Fiona's stubborn eyes.

"Keelin, if you do not take proper respect and let it be – you will be hurt or die. I can not be more serious about this point." Fiona's breath began to wheeze and Keelin realized that the old woman was starting to panic.

"Okay, okay. I got it. Respect the cove. I will do as you say." Keelin ran her hand gently down Fiona's arm. She would reserve her opinions on the cove for later.

"The cove has a long and varied history. I'm sure your mother filled you in on most of it. All I can say is that the cove has power. Whether the chalice lies there or not, the cove will reveal its secrets to whom it chooses. Some come here for help in becoming pregnant. Others come to take the water for healing those who are gravely ill. Only those who properly respect it will walk away unscathed. You can only enter these waters with a purity of purpose. Treasure hunters are often hurt or killed. Grace's Cove is as close as you can get to sacred waters. Grace O'Malley made her living on the water and while she was a ruthless woman, she pledged her heart to the sea, and the sea alone. Her greatest gift to it was coming to this cove and enchanting it. At the end of her life, she came here to rest in these waters."

Keelin had always loved folklore, especially those tales related to the sea. Pirates, sirens, and mythology always enraptured her and left her usually logical mind daydreaming for hours. She had a fiercely romantic side that often left her in tears.

"She came here to be at one with her only love she could trust – the sea," Keelin murmured. Her eyes pricked with a soft sheen of tears. There was something so very sad about how Grace O'Malley chose to end her life yet at the same time, it was strangely romantic. Keelin understood the call of the sea. The sea was a tempestuous woman, roughly angry one day, silkily soothing another. No other natural phenomenon reflected their moods as deeply as the sea. It was beauty. It was wrath. It was everything. Keelin could identify with Grace's last wish. To become a part of – one with – the sea was enchanting. Keelin's blood hummed at the thought.

Fiona led Keelin over a rocky path that wound through the pastures with the punk-rock sheep. The gentle breeze picked up speed as they neared the cove and the seabirds circled looking for their lunch. They approached the edge of a ledge and Keelin gasped as her soul sang.

Chapter Nine

THE COVE STRETCHED before them, its waters a crystal blue hugged by jagged cliffs. The steep cliffs cupped the water and allowed a small opening for boats in the exact middle of the cove. The cliffs tapered in a perfect half-circle, meeting at a small sand beach, hundreds of yards below them. A small path crossed the cliff below them, switch-backing down the steepness of the ledge. The cove was impossible in its beauty, untouched in its rawness, and so quietly alone. There should have been people on the beach, dogs running, and kids splashing in the water. Nothing marred the beauty of the beach. The birds flew over, never dipping into the water. The hum in Keelin's blood increased.

"Welcome to Grace's Cove. You'll be safe walking along the path. It isn't until you reach the beach that you should be concerned. We'll begin our protection at the beach."

"Grandma, do you hike this by yourself? This is not an easy climb." Keelin's breath huffed out as she began the walk down.

"Ah, you Americans. This is but a small walk. Try climbing Mt. Brandon if you'd like a nice hike." Fiona breezed on down, years of hiking the hills making her steps confident. Keelin followed more slowly. Her klutzy side was bound to make her trip and go rolling off the path to meet her death on the sharp rocks below.

Keelin watched as her grandmother gathered flowers on the way down. She kept up a constant lesson of various herbs and bushes, and Keelin began to notice that many of them were tied with ribbons.

"What are the ribbons for?" Keelin asked.

"I harvest herbs based on the moon and other astro-logical elements."

Keelin laughed.

Her grandmother stopped and looked at her. She shook her head and kept walking. Keelin could have sworn she heard her say, "There is more to heaven and earth, Horatio…"

"Shakespeare?" Keelin asked. Fiona nodded and kept walking.

"Okay, then." She blew out a breath and made a note not to laugh about the astrology stuff. She couldn't knock some of it. Even science had proven that the sea's tides were governed by the pull of the moon. Perhaps there was more to these forces than she knew. They approached the bottom of the path and Keelin steadied her breathing as the necklace hummed at her throat. Stepping from the path onto the warm sand, Fiona reached out a hand and stopped Keelin from proceeding further.

"No further. Just look." Fiona spread her hands out and turned. Her face creased into a smile and the sun shone its warm light onto her. She laughed and held her arms up to the sky, looking like a yogi doing a mountain pose.

The cove spread before them, infinite in its beauty. Here, the wind was sheltered and sun's rays were soft. The cliffs, which were so scary from above, cradled them, creating a feeling of safety. Keelin wanted to rip her clothes off and dive in and float in the effervescent waters. It was the most private of places, a piece of her, and she felt that she had come home.

"I know," Fiona said. "This is home."

"It – there are no words. I feel giddy," Keelin said. She wanted to dance naked on the sand. She could almost feel the cool caress of the water and the weightless feeling as she floated, unencumbered, and stared at the sky. Dizziness hit her, and she grabbed her water flask and took a sip to clear her head. Never had the call of the ocean hit her as hard as this.

"It calls to you. To anyone, actually. Those who are too weak often go running right in and are pulled out to sea. It beckons." Fiona nodded towards the water. "You must never go past this point without saying a prayer or giving an offering. Remember that."

Fiona pulled the bundles of flowers she had tied on the walk from her bag. With a small stick, she drew a circle in the sand and pulled Keelin into it with her.

"It is with purity of purpose, the greatest of admiration, and respect for the power here that we ask to enter the cove. As descendants of Grace O'Malley, we enter the cove with love, as is our birthright." Fiona laid the bundles of flowers outside the circle and handed a bunch to Keelin.

"Come, we can put these in the water as well." Fiona held her flowers in front of her and walked softly towards the water, pulling Keelin with her.

The water rippled towards them, coaxing them closer. Fiona laughed freely.

"It has such a mood. A siren's song, if you will. Many who come here are lost to it. It will be nice to us though. We've brought the appropriate gifts and it will be happy that you are home," Fiona said. Together, they flung the flowers far into the water. Keelin felt happiness pierce her heart as she watched the blooms flutter down to the water, where they rested gently on the waves.

Fiona peeled off her boots and, laughing with abandon, ran to the water's edge. She threw another bouquet of flowers into the air and they split, showering down onto a wave that reached up to catch them. Mesmerized by the sight, Keelin stood frozen.

"Come, Keelin!"

Keelin raced to the water. She skidded to a stop next to Fiona and let the water caress her ankles. Grains of sand squished between her toes and the sun warmed her shoulders. The feelings were intoxicating. Keelin never wanted to leave.

"Let me show you my favorite spots," Fiona said, eagerly pulling Keelin down the shoreline. Fiona stopped in front of a small cluster of rocks that formed a tidal pool with about six inches of clear water. Keelin could make out small fish darting between the rocks, and thin strands of a bright green sea grass waved in the water. Fiona bent and culled some of the grass and placed it in a small jar with seawater.

"This is the best stuff for the face creams that I make. Something about this particular sea grass works better than any other I have seen," Fiona explained. Keelin looked at the lines around Fiona's eyes and realized that she really did look far more youthful than her eighty years would suggest.

"I'm allowed to use my knowledge for some vanity, you know." Fiona winked at Keelin and she laughed. Fiona spent the afternoon showing Keelin nooks and crannies, tidal pools filled with interesting sea life, certain seaweeds and moss for healing, and various plants that grew along the water's edge.

"Is it safe to swim? I can't see any undercurrents from the surface," Keelin asked. She was dying to get in the water.

"Yes, it is, but I will wait on the shore for you. I want to tie up the plants that I collected."

Stripping to her bra and underwear, Keelin dove in with abandon. The cool water slipped over her skin and she dove deep, waiting for her favorite part – the feeling of weightlessness. As she hung, suspended, Keelin turned on her back and looked up towards the sky. The salt stung her eyes, yet she could never resist cracking her eyes just once, looking up at the sky and watching her bubbles of air float over her. These moments hung still, almost timeless, and were her favorite part of being in the sea. She swam to the surface and broke free, laughing.

"It's so beautiful here!" She swam in towards the beach and walked out of the water. Her underwear clung to her like a second skin and she bent over and shook out her long hair. Wringing the water out, she stood up in time to see Fiona waving at something behind her. Keelin jumped and turned in time to see a small boat in the cove and the familiar glint of blue eyes gleaming at her. She saw the flash of a bright smile and heat flushed up her body. Her wet bra and underwear left nothing to the imagination and Flynn made a slow perusal of her body. His dog raced back and forth in the boat with him and barked excitedly as Flynn pulled a net in. Flynn sent her a jaunty wave.

Keelin gave him the finger and stormed back up the beach.

"I thought nobody could come in the cove," Keelin steamed to Fiona as she pulled her t-shirt over her wet clothes. She was furious that Flynn had caught her at a disadvantage again.

"I said people who were searching for treasure or didn't protect themselves. Flynn learned long ago the ways of the cove. His respect is rewarded in the freshest of seafood and he gets premium prices for what he catches from here."

"Hmpf." Keelin glared at him over the water. That man showed up at the damndest of times.

With a small smile, Fiona hummed a song and gathered her finds for the day.

"Come, let's go eat. I'm famished. Perhaps we can ride into town for a pint."

Keelin nodded her agreement. Quickly, she gathered her goods and refused to look back at the small boat on the cove. She had given Flynn enough satisfaction for the day.

Chapter Ten

FIONA WARMED UP an Irish stew and brown bread for dinner. Starving, Keelin found herself asking for seconds. She made a note to pay attention to what she ate here. All this brown bread could not be good for her waistline. She sighed. Not like she had the best waistline as it was, but her soft curves still showed a nice hourglass figure. Keelin blushed at thinking of Flynn seeing her in her underwear. Usually she wore a one-piece and a cover-up at the pool.

"Grandma, can you tell me about my father? Is he still here? Mom won't talk of him."

It had been on Keelin's mind all day and she hadn't known the best way to bring it up. Keelin typically went the direct route with these things so she decided to spring it on Fiona.

"Yes, I know your father. He no longer lives in Grace's Cove. The poor man really struggled after your mother left. He did eventually marry and have children though."

"Excuse me? Children? I have brothers or sisters?" Keelin said. Her hand slammed the plate she was holding to the table and she struggled to take a breath. Her mother had never said a word. Keelin's heart pounded as she thought of seeing siblings that looked like her.

"Well, yes. Did you think that he never moved on? Why hasn't your mother told you this?" Fiona *tsk-tsked* as she cleared the table. "You have a half-sister and a half-brother. Twins. They still live here. Your father lives in Dublin. I suppose it will only be right for me to take you to meet them." Fiona smoothed the cloth that she had dried the dishes with.

"I, I. I don't even know what to say. A brother and a sister." Keelin felt tears prick her eyes at the injustice of not knowing about her family. She had always wanted siblings. Fiona crossed to her and gently rubbed her arm. Keelin could feel a cool balm course through her from Fiona's touch.

"Let's go down for a pint. You look like you need a drink. We can talk more."

Keelin, still reeling from the surprise of not being an only child, stumbled her way into her room to change into fresh clothes. How could Fiona have told her this news so casually? She truly must have thought that Margaret told her about the twins. Keelin made a mental note to have a serious word with her mother. She wondered what other

73

secrets she would uncover during her stay. Keelin glanced quickly at her phone to see that there were no missed calls. Margaret hadn't called yet to check in with her. Keelin sighed and moved to her closet.

What to wear to an Irish pub? Not sure of the dress code in a small village, she pulled on a maxi skirt, boots, and a black scoop-neck top. She topped the outfit off with a statement necklace, left her long hair to curl loosely in beachy waves from the sea salt, and added some mascara to make her eyes pop. This was as good as it would get after a day like today, she thought. Ancient pirates, healers, universal powers, protection prayers, and the addition of new family members was enough to make her want to curl up in bed with her iPad and a bucket of ice cream.

Keelin found Fiona in front of the cottage in a late-model cherry-red SUV. She looked stylish with her hair tamed in a braid, wearing a white blouse tucked into a navy skirt with flowers embroidered at the hem. Silver drops winked at her ears and Keelin could see a necklace of intricate crystals around her neck.

"Come on! Girl's night!" Fiona laughed at her.

Smiling, Keelin hopped in and watched as the sun tucked itself into the horizon. The cliffs turned crimson in the soft light and the cove took on a dreamlike quality. If she painted, Keelin would do it in watercolor and call it "Goodnight Kiss."

"Tell me about my brother and sister," Keelin said. The words felt weird. She had always wished for a sister or brother but had certainly not expected to discover a pair of siblings this late in life.

"Your father was devastated after your mother left, but like most men, he didn't function well on his own. He went looking for someone to fill her place and eventually settled with a quiet young woman from the neighboring village. Your sister and brother were born quite quickly after their wedding and we aren't entirely sure if a full nine months had passed, if you get my meaning. Though, I hear that twins come early."

"How old are they?"

"Hmm, let's see, this was two years after your mother left. So I'd say 26 or 27? A couple of years younger than you."

"Where do they live?"

"They are both in the village; your brother helps to run the local chemist in the next town over and your sister has an art studio downtown."

Keelin wondered if it was the storefront with the lace that she had stopped to admire.

"Their names?" Keelin asked quietly.

"Oh my! Yes, of course. Colin and Aislinn. Fine Irish names." Fiona pulled into a small lot behind a brightly colored pub. A cheerful red door complemented the deep blue of the building, and the sound of a pipe lilted through the open door.

"Ahh, the first set is starting," Fiona said.

Keelin noticed the rough-hewn sign with the deeply etched "Gallagher's Pub" that hung over the door. She hoped this was the same pub that the nice girl she had met at the airport owned. She assumed it was. Just how many Gallagher's Pubs would there be in this village?

Keelin walked into the pub and scanned the room. Booths were crammed with families, and people of all ages laughed and jostled each other as they clapped along with the band that was tucked into a small booth in front. The walls were cluttered with family photos, the path was clear to the bar, and the lighting was just right to complement the females of the place. Keelin followed Fiona as she wove her way to the bar, and noticed some people quickly step out of her way and cross themselves. Others greeted Fiona with a shout.

"Two Bulmers, please." Fiona ordered for her. "You'll love the local cider. Crisp and refreshing after a day like today."

Keelin nodded. She preferred dark beer, but a cider did sound refreshing. Her neck tingled. She turned her head and saw the flash of blue eyes that seemed to follow her. Flynn sat in the middle of the booth and strummed a cheerful tune on his banjo, matching his deep baritone to the lilting soprano in the group. His large hands caressed the banjo lovingly and Keelin found herself mesmerized by the way he stroked the instrument. His fingers played lightly across the strings and she imagined his hands on her. Cursing herself, she flushed as his eyes met hers and he cracked a smile. Damn that man. Of course he played an instrument too. Was there anything he couldn't do?

Keelin gulped down half of her cider and followed her grandmother to a small table. Keelin was introduced to a few of the locals. She scanned the room and hoped to see Cait.

"Hello."

Keelin turned and saw a blond man standing by her table. He was tall and lanky and was just saved from boyishness by a stubborn jut to his jaw. His brown eyes were nice, yet his smile didn't fully reach his eyes.

"I'm Shane MacAuliffe. You must be Fiona's granddaughter, Keelin." He held out his hand.

"Yes, hello. Nice to meet you." Keelin held out her hand. Shane held it a beat longer than was polite and Keelin saw healthy male admiration in his eyes. She allowed her smile to deepen. What a perfect distraction this could be from the surly male tucked in the front booth.

"Join us, please." Keelin patted a spot on the bench next to her. She noticed Fiona didn't address Shane, but she was engaged in conversation with people to her right.

"I'd love to, thank you." Shane sat close to Keelin and began to quiz her about the States. He spoke longingly of the freedom of big towns and Keelin wondered if he yearned for more than what Grace's Cove offered to him. His brown eyes took on a sense of anticipation as he hung on Keelin's words about Boston.

On her second round of cider, Keelin laughed at Shane. "Enough about me! Tell me about yourself." Keelin had noticed that not many people in the pub had spoken with Shane, though he had waved at many. Something was off

77

here. A flash of bitterness crossed his face and then his features smoothed.

"I work here in town. I'm in commercial real estate and own many of the business properties downtown. As a landlord, I guess you could say that I'm not the most popular guy in a town that struggles to make rent." He produced a sheepish grin with the statement and looked at her from under his eyebrows.

Keelin was charmed. Her mother would love Shane. Which meant Keelin could never date him. No harm making friends though, she thought. Shane proceeded to point people out around the bar and regale her with local lore. She found herself laughing and enjoying his company. He wasn't such a bad guy. Risking a look, she glanced towards the musicians in the front booth. The smug smile gone, Flynn met her eyes directly. Not my problem, she thought. She wanted nothing to do with him. She lifted her chin and looked away.

"Keelin!" Cait waved to her from behind the bar. The band was on break and Keelin excused herself to go say hello to Cait. Cait looked petite behind the bar but managed to keep conversations going as she topped off three glasses of Guinness that waited to settle and poured a whiskey neat.

"How are you settling in?" Cait asked.

"I'm doing good. It's really been a whirlwind. I'm learning a lot. Like way too much." The cider was catching up with her a bit and Keelin bit down on her lip before she said something revealing.

"Well, I've earned myself a break. Let's have a sip of whiskey to commemorate your arrival and you can tell me what you were talking with Shane about. He seems to like you."

Keelin caught a hint of bitterness there.

"No, no. He's just a nice guy talking to me about the town."

"Mmm." Cait made a noncommittal noise and eased herself under the pass-through. Nudging a few guys out of the way, she cleared a spot for Keelin and her to sit at a high table in the back.

"Do you have a boyfriend?" Cait asked her as she raised her glass to Keelin in a toast.

"No, I'm single. I have been for a while to be honest. Boston guys just want quick one-night stands and I'm just not into that." Keelin couldn't bring herself to say that they didn't want one-night stands with her – the bigger girl who had a hint of something off about her. She just never seemed to manage herself well in normal relationships.

"Well, men are nothing but trouble anyway and I've sworn myself off them. For a while at least." Cait laughed at her but Keelin saw her watch Shane as she said that.

"Trouble they are." Keelin glanced quickly to the front booth, but Flynn was gone. Shrugging, she returned to the conversation.

"So, you found out about Colin and Aislinn, I'm as-suming?" Being a bartender had taught Cait to cut to the quick of things.

"Whoa. Yes, holy shit. I mean, how do I just go through twenty-eight years of not knowing that I have a sister and a brother?" Keelin slammed her hand flat on the table. "I mean, come on!"

"No kidding. Someone should have told you. They knew about you. It's only fair." Holding up her whiskey in commiseration, Cait clinked her glass to Keelin's.

Keelin couldn't believe it. She sputtered against the heat of the whiskey.

"They knew about me! Why didn't they try to contact me?" She took down the rest of her whiskey in one gulp and coughed as it burned her throat. Cait pumped her on the back and laughed.

"Slow down. It's meant for sipping."

Tears pricked Keelin's eyes as she struggled to breathe. She took a tentative sip of her cider to cool her throat.

"I don't know why they didn't get hold of you. It was all so long ago and we all knew that Margaret would never come back. It just didn't seem real until you showed up," Cait said.

Keelin nodded. She supposed it made sense. But that wasn't going to stop her from having some choice words with her mother.

"My break's over. Next set is starting soon. Come see me for lunch this week. I'd love to have a girl's night soon." Cait smiled and cleared the table as she shouted to the bartenders to get moving.

Keelin nodded and stood up to go, catching her foot on the stool and tipping a bit as she stumbled forward directly into a rock-hard chest. Lifting her eyes up, she blew hair out of her eyes as she stared at a dreamy mouth a few inches from hers. Blue eyes looked into hers.

"Steady as you go there. Perhaps you should slow down on the liquor," Flynn said as he gripped her arms.

"Perhaps you should not tell me what to do," Keelin said, and pushed his hands off of her arms. She stomped past him back to her table, cursing herself for the flush that crept up her face and how close she had been to leaning in and taking a little nip of his lip. Just a small tug of that deep bottom lip. A long, liquid pull tugged low in her stomach. Keelin groaned. She did need to lay off the liquor or she'd be throwing herself at Flynn in no time.

Shane quickly joined her at the table and nudged a glass of water towards her.

"I saw Cait shoving whiskey at you," Shane said. He sliced an accusatory glance at the bar.

"No, she wasn't shoving. We were toasting. The new additions to my family, apparently." Keelin giggled.

"Oh, your sister and brother? Yes, I suppose that was a shock if you didn't know," Shane said.

"Jesus, does anyone not know everyone's business here?" Keelin wondered.

"Small Irish towns. Long history. You'll get used to hearing the same stories over and over," Shane said with a shrug.

"I suppose."

"Say, Keelin." Shane leaned closer and put his hand on her leg. "I'd love to take you to dinner sometime if you'd be interested." He smiled and looked into her eyes. His meaning was clear. Her mind wasn't.

"Um, sure, maybe. Well, as friends. I'm not really looking to date anyone at the moment." Keelin saw Cait throw her towel down on the bar and storm off. She looked up and saw Flynn glaring at her from the front booth.

"Friends. Just as friends." Shane smiled. "I'd like that." He leaned over and pecked her on the cheek and Keelin blushed.

"Time to go, Keelin." Fiona grabbed her hand and helped her up. She was softly singing to the music and entwined her arms with hers as she walked out. Stars pricked the sky and a breeze teased the ocean scent to her.

"So you like that young Shane, do you?" Fiona asked as she started the car and drove from the harbor and towards the hills.

"He seemed nice. But I think Cait's into him. He asked me out on a date. My mother would love him – a prosperous real estate owner."

"Hmm, and will you go?"

"No." Keelin sighed. "I learned long ago that if my mother would love him then I will hate him. It just doesn't work. Plus, I'd like to be friends with Cait and it seems like the waters are muddy there."

"That's a good girl."

Fiona pulled the car into the drive. They chattered about the local gossip on the way into the house. Fiona stopped and gave Keelin a hug in the kitchen.

"I'm so happy you are here. It's been lonely." She smiled and gave Keelin a scone, along with a pitcher of water for her room. "Sleep well, dear."

Keelin wolfed down the scone and then cursed herself. So much for watching the calories. She poured a glass of water and walked to the window, looking out over the cove. It was hypnotizing in the moonlight. The sky spread over the water and the stars looked like someone had tossed a bag of diamonds onto a velvet rug. It was so hauntingly beautiful that she was compelled to go outside to see it more clearly.

Keelin quietly eased the latch open and snuck out of the house. Not that she had to sneak out, she reminded herself. She was a twenty-eight-year-old woman and she could damn well go outside if she wanted to look at the stars.

The sound of waves pulled her towards the cove. The sky was stunning and the moon's light sliced a path through the water. Until the cove. It stopped at the cove. Keelin was determined to see why this was and hurried her way across the hills until she reached the edge of the cove. The waters remained dark though the moon shone brightly above them. Keelin rushed down the path to the shore, slipping and sliding on the rough trail, the cider making her clumsier than usual. At the base of the path, she stumbled onto the beach.

"I don't get it. How does this make sense?" She walked rapidly towards the cove, scanning the cliffs to see where the light of the moon ended. The beach was lit up, yet the water remained dark.

"This just shouldn't be."

She walked towards the edge of the water. Was there something in the water that prevented reflection? A type of reverse phosphorous fish that absorbed the light? She reached down at the water's edge to scoop up a handful of water and sand to check if the water held something unusual…perhaps a dark substance of sorts. A huge crash sounded and she was hit hard with a wave. The force of the water dragged her across the bottom of the sand and her leg sliced against coral. Keelin shrieked and closed her mouth against the onslaught of water and held her breath. She was tumbled across the sand of the beach and scrambled to catch her feet in the fierce undertow. Her long skirt wound between her legs and her boots made her clumsy. She tried to kick for the surface when she was jerked from the water and dragged against a hard chest.

Keelin gasped for air and held on as she was pulled onto the beach. She tripped over her feet and skirt and was scooped up as if she weighed nothing. She coughed out water and nestled into the warmth of the chest. Just for a moment. She knew who had rescued her. She needed a moment.

Unfortunately, a moment she would not get.

Flynn dropped Keelin to her feet.

"Of all the stupid things to do this has to be the dumbest of the dumb. I thought you were some fancy marine science girl and you go into the water, alone, after drinking.

In water that you don't know anything about? Could you be any more stupid? I can't believe you would even take a risk like this. I should have Fiona chain you to your bed at night," Flynn raged at her.

"Stupid?" Keelin hated being called stupid. Her Irish temper kicked in. "Who are you calling stupid, you big oaf? What are you doing down here anyway?"

She pounded her fist on his chest and he grabbed her wrist with his hand. His eyes glinted dangerously at her as he held her hand captive.

"Obviously, I'm saving a stupid child from drowning."

"A child? You, you jerk. Leave me alone." She spun away to stomp off and was whipped back. Keelin found herself plastered against his hard chest. She huffed out a breath and tried to calm her hammering heart.

"Let me go!" Keelin's eyes met his in the moonlight. Her nipples tightened against his chest. Keelin sucked in a breath as she saw his eyes dilate and narrow. Her heart skipped a beat and the moment held for a second. Flynn cursed and crushed her to him and took her lips with his. He nipped at her bottom lip, angry, yet oh-so-gentle. She moaned. His tongue slipped between her lips, dipping, diving, mimicking a gentle rhythm. Enticing her. She tasted whiskey and the sea. It was a heady mix and much like the sea, it pulled her under. Suddenly desperate, she ran her hands up his strong shoulders and threaded them through his thick hair. His mouth assaulted hers mercilessly, and he hitched her up so her legs wound around his waist, her skirt pushed to her thighs. She sucked at his bottom lip and ground herself against him. She felt helpless, yet impossibly turned on by the way he carried her. Keelin could feel his hard length pressed against her most intimate of spots. He was just as lost as she was.

Flynn kneeled in the sand and laid her down, cradling her in his arms as he pressed a knee between her legs. Craving more, Keelin rubbed against the pressure of his leg as he continued his assault on her mouth. It had been so long since she'd felt such passion. In fact, she'd never felt like this before. Liquid heat pooled in her stomach and she wanted him to touch every part of her. His strong hands slipped beneath her shirt and skimmed up her sides. Her breath caught as he slipped a hand inside her bra, cradling her wet breast that was grainy with sand. His warm hand rubbed the sand against her cold nipples and heat shot straight to her belly.

Keelin moaned deeply as the sensations began to build within her. She writhed against his leg as he continued to rub her nipples, over and over, round and round, his tongue flicking in and out of her mouth, dipping his head to nuzzle at a sensitive spot on her neck. Keelin felt the pressure building and opened her eyes as he pulled her into his lap and trailed his hand up her leg. Flynn pulled back and met her eyes just as he slid a finger deep inside of her. Keelin exploded and buried her face in his shoulder as she convulsed around his hand. Her body shook with the tremors and she raised her head to catch a breath and gasped as the cove glowed blue from within.

"What, wait, stop. Stop!" Keelin struggled for breath and her sanity. She stumbled back off of Flynn. Flynn sat back on his knees and ran his hand through his messy hair, breathing hard. His eyes bored into hers.

"You took advantage of me!" Keelin yelled. She wasn't sure why she said it but she was still reeling from the sight of the now dark cove being lit from within. She must be losing her mind.

"I did no such thing. You wanted that and you know it. It's not my fault you're wound so tight that you go off at the slightest touch."

"You bastard." Keelin gathered what little dignity she had and stormed towards the cliff path.

"Ouch!" She stopped and looked down at her leg. She pulled her wet skirt up and saw blood leaking from a large gash in her leg. Vaguely she remembered the scrape of coral on her leg before muscular arms had wrapped around her.

"Damn it." Keelin heard Flynn curse seconds before she was lifted into his arms.

"Don't! I can walk. I don't need you to take care of me," Keelin protested, pushing at the wall of his chest as he climbed the path.

"Stop pushing me or I will throw you over my shoulder like a sack of potatoes."

"You wouldn't dare! Put me down!" Keelin was in full Irish temper.

"Damn it, woman, you are nothing but a headache." Flynn unceremoniously lifted her and dumped her over his shoulder, locking his arm firmly under her butt. Keelin blushed in shame and smacked him on his firm behind.

He laughed.

Keelin sighed and stopped. She craned her neck to look at the cove and swore she could still see a faint blue shimmer deep in the water. She focused on regulating her breathing and tried to bring her temper down. Letting her science brain click in, she tried to configure a list of reasons for why the cove would have glowed blue. From within. At the exact moment she lost her senses to his touch.

Keelin flushed. Her insides were still singing and she could feel heat everywhere that he touched her. Why was she so attracted to him? He was surly, rude, and blew her off. Not to mention the fact that he only saw her in awkward or compromising positions. Just once she would like to have the upper hand with him. Keelin squirmed on his shoulder and felt the heat of his hand pressed hard into her legs. Everywhere their bodies touched hummed with energy. It was as though the universal power of attraction was meant just for them. Keelin wondered if there was some sort of "power" he had that she was tuned to.

She turned and smacked him on the head. "Are you a wizard?"

"Jesus, Keelin, are you drunk?" Flynn muttered about crazy women and reached the front of the cottage. He gently placed her down, though she was sure that he wanted to throw her in the gravel path. He crouched and lifted her skirt, revealing the deep gash.

"Just hold on a minute, okay?" Flynn asked. Keelin nodded quietly. His touch on her leg was taking her mind far from the pain. He opened a small pouch and placed an ointment on her leg. A cooling sensation immediately relieved the pain. Surprised, she sat up and stared at him.

"What is that?" Keelin demanded. She knew that coral cuts typically stung for far longer than a normal cut, as coral would often have a poison that could irritate the skin for days.

Flynn smiled as he pocketed the jar.

"Ask your grandmother."

"Ah, I see." Keelin looked at him quietly. What was there to say? The day caught up with her and exhaustion hit. Part of her wanted to weep. It was just too much. Weird powers, a new family, a foreign country, and now Flynn.

"Don't. Are you going to cry? Does it hurt? Come on now. Where's the feisty girl that was spitting like a wet cat just moments ago?"

Flynn ran his hands through his hair and managed to look supremely frustrated and concerned at the same time.

"I just. This. All of it. What am I even doing here? This is too much. I can't have family that I didn't know about. And I know Fiona looks at me to carry on her legacy. And this. You. What, I don't even know what is. And why did the cove glow blue? Did you see that? That's not even normal. I think I'm losing it." Keelin babbled on, wringing her hands in her lap. She reached to her hair and began braiding it, an old habit of hers to calm herself when she was stressed.

"Glowed blue? You saw the cove glow?" Flynn cut through everything else and focused on that one point.

"Yes, it was blue. Right when I, you know. When, um." Keelin blushed.

"When I slipped my hand into you and you lost yourself?" Flynn supplied helpfully, moving towards her slowly, a predatory look in his eyes.

"Yes! No. I mean yes, but no to you coming any closer. I mean it, Flynn, back off." Keelin had had all she could take. "I should really just go home. This is all ridiculous. Thanks for carrying me up but I need to go to bed."

Keelin turned away without looking at him. She wasn't prepared to answer any of the questions he had. She needed to ask Fiona about the light in the cove. But for now, she needed to be alone. Closing the door quietly behind her, she tiptoed to her room. A small light was switched on by her bed, along with a tray on the table. The tray held a scone, cold tea, and a pile of bandages and ointment.

"How did she even know?" Keelin whispered. Exhausted, and beyond trying to figure out the events of the day, Keelin stripped and showered the sand off her. Leaving her hair bundled in a towel, she bandaged her leg and crawled into bed. She would look into flights back to Boston in the morning.

Chapter Eleven

KEELIN AWOKE TO bright light. Her shades had been opened and the sun was far from the horizon. Dizzy, she patted the bed for her phone. She clicked it on and saw it was already late morning.

Keelin sighed and sat back as the events of the night before washed over her. She blushed as images of Flynn's mouth and the taste of him flashed through her. The man had the mouth of a god. She tried not to think about how quickly she had gone off in his hands and thought it was best not to dwell on it. It was probably just a fluke. It had been a long time for her was all. Adding to that some whiskey, the adrenaline from the cove being insane, and Flynn rescuing her, she supposed it would make her more susceptible to his touch. She wouldn't be able to look him in the face anytime soon, of course, but as she planned to go back to Boston anyway, she doubted that it mattered much. They were consensual adults. Mature people. No biggie, right?

Keelin examined her cut and was amazed to see how healthy it looked. The bright red and puckered skin of the night before had faded to a light pink and the skin had healed up nicely. Witch or no witch, Fiona clearly knew her stuff when it came to ointments.

Keelin pulled out her iPad and looked up flights home. There were flights that flew to Boston almost daily from Shannon. She hesitated before purchasing one. She owed Fiona a conversation first. And, Keelin thought, she might have a little more to learn about healing. The thought of fully embracing her healing abilities intrigued her and she would be stupid not to try to learn from the best. Keelin thought of her mother. Margaret had denied what she was and only used her ability to read people to make sales. Part of her was very happy with her success and part of her seemed deeply unhappy. Keelin had to wonder if it was because Margaret had never fully explored what she was.

Mulling over these thoughts, Keelin pulled on walking shorts and a tank in acknowledgement of the bright sunshine poking through the window. She checked the waters of the cove. It looked peaceful this morning and Keelin was determined to take her dive gear down to the cove today and begin some studies of the underwater life. If the cove accepted her, that was. Keelin had been sincerely shocked last night when the huge wave had hit her. There was no possible way that gentle waters had turned into a freak wave. There was no science to explain what had happened and it didn't sit comfortably with Keelin. Not to mention that blue glow. Keelin shook her head and headed into the kitchen to make a much-needed cup of tea.

Keelin found a note by some fruit and brown bread. Fiona had gone to the village for some supplies and would be back in early afternoon. Probably for the best, Keelin thought. She needed a morning to wallow in thoughts about her additional family members and what she should do with her life direction.

A knock at the door startled her. Grumbling, she pushed her unruly bed hair from her face, and opened the door. A large basket sat before her with a bow. She quickly looked up. Flynn's dog sat on the ridge overlooking the house, watching her. Flynn was nowhere to be seen. In fact, there was nobody to be seen anywhere. Keelin strained her ears but did not hear the sounds of a car leaving.

"Hmpf," Keelin said. She jumped as a series of yips came from the basket and it upended on its side. A puppy tumbled out, roughly six months or so, a roly-poly black-and-white setter. It saw her and excitedly yipped and ran in circles around her. Charmed, she leaned down to pet it. A note was attached to the basket. Keelin unfolded it and read the words out loud.

"My sincerest apologies if I "took advantage" of you last night. Though I don't think that was the case, I would like to offer you a gift that will keep you company and watch out for you, as you clearly need watching over."

Keelin flushed. She felt ashamed. She shouldn't have said that Flynn had taken advantage of her. Once he had kissed her she had all but crawled all over him. It hadn't been fair of her to accuse him of that and it was clear his honor was offended.

She looked down at the dog. It wriggled towards her on its belly in the grass. Keelin couldn't help but smile. It was a really cute puppy.

"But, a dog?" Keelin said. She knew the responsibility that a dog carried. Flynn was forcing her to make a choice. If she kept the dog she would need to stay here. If she didn't, she was free to go home. Damn that man for forcing her hand. How could someone she had just met annoy her and intrigue her as much as Flynn did?

Keelin watched the dog, charmed despite herself. She was a little pissed at Flynn for forcing this choice on her, especially the morning after the emotional events of yesterday. Thoughts of her life in Boston wound through her head – an empty apartment, her friends, school, the aquarium, and her mother. Her mother would want her to come home, finish her master's degree, and settle down with a nice boy who was either a doctor or a lawyer. Keelin sat in the grass and pet the puppy. He yipped excitedly and rolled on his back, begging for stomach scratches. She smiled at his enthusiasm and allowed the sun to warm her back. It was peaceful here, the quiet crash of the waves a constant song in the background.

"Oh, you're a real pushover, aren't you?" She laughed down at the pup. Keelin thought about how empty she had felt in Boston. Maybe not empty, but just unfinished. A part of her had always felt set apart, as though she didn't fit there no matter how hard she tried. Keelin had experienced more true feelings in one week in Ireland than she had in years in Boston. She felt like a Band-Aid had been ripped off. It was like she had been emotionally stunted and everything was pouring out now. The intensity scared her, yet at the same time challenged her. Keelin rarely resisted a challenge. She imagined her mom's reaction when she told her she would be turning her summer vacation in Ireland to an indefinite stay. She shook her head. That would be a difficult conversation she would have to shelve for later.

Sighing, she picked the puppy up.

"Okay, boy. Looks like you are for me. Let's get you some food." Keelin looked up to see Flynn's dog bob its head at her and disappear over the ridge.

"This is just weird." Keelin shook her head and picked up the basket to find a blanket, a supply of food, and a dog brush. That man thought of everything. A small smile tugged at her lips. She'd always wanted a puppy.

She carried the puppy inside and laughed as it ran around the room, sniffing corners and barking at imaginary threats. She hoped Fiona would be okay with their new companion. Keelin dug through some drawers and found a long piece of rope and went to change into her swimming suit. Picking up her fins and snorkel gear, she called to the pup.

"Let's go for a walk, buddy." She'd have to think of a fine Irish name for the puppy. Leaving a note for Fiona, she latched the door and made her way across the fields towards the cove. It was time to get in the water and begin her research. The puppy raced ahead of her, yipping and jumping at bugs. She whistled for him and he circled back to her, yapping ecstatically at her feet. Smart dog, she thought.

"I'm going to name you Ronan," Keelin said. Having take care of that matter, she made her way to the cliff's edge. The puppy stopped at her feet and trembled, looking down. It was a big hike for a little guy, so she picked Ronan up and headed down the path. Ronan licked her face happily and then, as puppies do, fell asleep in her arms.

Reaching the bottom of the cliff path, Keelin looked around for an appropriate spot to get Ronan set up while she was in the water. She started across the sand towards a small tree that was sheltered in a rocky outcropping. She could tie Ronan to the tree and he would have shade while he slept.

Keelin cursed. Stopped. And walked back a few steps. She laid Ronan gently down on the sand and pulled out a few flowers and pretty stones she had gathered on the walk down. Tracing a circle around Ronan and herself, she cleared her throat.

"Um, hi, Grace's Cove. I'd like to offer you these gifts that I have brought for you today." She placed some flowers on the sand and hurled the pretty stones into the water. She tried desperately to remember everything that Fiona had told her about entering the cove. Purity of purpose, she remembered.

"I am simply here to observe your beautiful waters and to document the plants and animals found underwater for my thesis. Research is just part of what I do. I, um, ask the universe and my angels for protection while I am here, oh, and to protect Ronan too!" Keelin made the sign of the cross for good measure. She squinted at the cove but nothing had changed.

"Well, here goes nothing." Keelin hoped that she had made the appropriate gestures and headed towards the rocky outcropping. She tied Ronan up and laid him down on her towel, along with a small hunk of rope to chew on. The exhausted puppy curled up and watched her through one eye.

Keelin pulled her mask and fins out of the bag and made her way to the water. Today would be a free diving day without tanks. Tanks were too heavy to lug down here anyway, she thought. She would need to bring them on a boat if she wanted to do any serious diving. Spitting in her mask to keep it from fogging up, she entered the water and cleared the mask out. Keelin scooped some water in her hand and tamed her hair back from her face and adjusted her mask over her head. She turned her back to the water and walked backwards against the waves, bending over to tuck a fin on each foot. She squinted through her mask and could have sworn she saw Flynn's dog racing across the cliffs above the cove.

That's weird, she thought. Didn't his dog typically go fishing with him? She shrugged and rolled facedown into the water. A kaleidoscope of colors flashed before her as a group of fish swam past her. She smiled into her snorkel. This was home to her.

Breathing easily, Keelin allowed herself to just float. She had no agenda with this dive other than to get her bearings, examine the ocean floor, and begin to learn the pattern of the cove. She stayed in the shallow waters and examined some of her favorite things, small mounds of coral that housed the tiniest of crustacean and fish communities. They always made her laugh and she entertained herself by imagining personalities for all of the small creatures that thrived on these bits of living rock.

A glimpse of light caught her eye, and Keelin turned towards darker water. She could have sworn that she had seen a flash of gold. She kicked with her powerful fins and quickly propelled herself towards where she had seen the glint. In deeper water now, Keelin strained her eyes as the light struggled to reach the bottom of the ocean. Visibility was less here as the waves hitting the rocky outcroppings of the shore churned sand back up. Taking a deep breath, Keelin dove down to get closer to the lump of coral that lay below her. She hovered around it and examined the coral for unusual lumps. Typically, any type of metal or lost "treasure" would have coral grown around it or have a small community of mussels attached to it. It would be easy to miss. Unable to hold her breath any longer, Keelin swam towards the surface and caught another glimpse of gold further out. Swearing, she broke the surface and dove down immediately without checking her position, as she didn't want to lose her bearing on the gold.

She swam further out and the bottom grew more distant. Where had she seen that gold glint? Suddenly realizing just how far the bottom was from her, Keelin gasped. She had unintentionally violated the number one rule of diving – plan your dive and dive your plan. She could see the particles in the water moving fast past her and realized she had crossed into a current. Cursing herself, Keelin popped her head out of the water and could see Ronan barking hysterically at then end of his rope – a tiny dot on the beach. Looking up, she saw the curve of the entrance to the cove rapidly passing her. She was being swept out to sea.

Keelin swore and forced herself to breathe slowly. She put her face back in the water and made herself horizontal. She was a trained diver and had handled currents before. The key was not to panic. Struggling against the current, Keelin kicked against it, trying to cut across the current and not into it. If she could just make it across the current, she would be out of it and fine. It seemed to be coming at her from all directions and she struggled at finding which way to kick. Panic began to grip her.

Dimly, she heard the sound of a motor. Keelin popped her head out of water and raised her arms in the universal sign for help.

"Help! Help me!" she screeched, and then shoved the snorkel back in her mouth as water clogged her throat.

Breathe, just breathe, she thought. She kept the snorkel in and continued to yell through it, waving her arms. The boat turned towards her and quickly picked up speed.

Keelin placed her head back in the water to make her breathing easier and held one arm out of the water so the boat could see her. She stared at the bottom of the ocean and could have sworn she saw a dull blue light. She must be hallucinating.

The motor cut and strong arms grabbed her. Huffing out salt water, Keelin dragged herself over the side of the boat and collapsed facedown. Her body shook with small tremors and she allowed the adrenaline to hit her. Her teeth chattered and she pushed the mask off of her face and stared into Flynn's blue eyes.

"I suppose I should thank you," Keelin stuttered. She tried to regain her composure as she lifted her chin at him.

"Of all the…how do I end up with the woman that is stubborn as all get-out?" Flynn said to himself as he started the motor and whipped towards shore. Keelin pulled the towel that he had handed around her and tried to get warm.

"You know, most women would have thrown themselves on me in gratitude. You know, promising anything I wanted? Offers of undying devotion? Baked goods? No. You can barely thank me." Flynn glared at her.

Keelin stared regally at him from across the boat.

"I am sure I would have been fine. I just needed to cut across the current is all, and I was a bit disorientated."

"A bit? You were a quarter mile out! You were shark bait. A goner! What were you even thinking? Are you insane?" Flynn lost it as they motored quietly into the cove. His shouts echoed off the walls of the empty cove and Ronan went silent on the beach.

"Hey! You aren't the boss of me! I'll have you know that I am a trained diver. I study this. This is what I do."

"Trained? Hardly! If you were trained you would know not to go diving alone and perhaps maybe to study the waters ahead of time and know that there is a nine-knot current that runs outside the cove. Had I not been out fishing today and heard your cry for help you would have been gone in minutes!" Flynn cut the motor and raged at her.

Keelin stood up on shaky legs and yelled at him.

"I'll have you know that I am a professional!"

"A professional pain in the ass!"

They were nose to nose in the rocking boat. Keelin's breath huffed out and her chest heaved.

Flynn sighed and laid his forehead against hers, surprising her.

"Just. Just don't ever do that again. Please."

Chagrined, she nodded.

"I could use a hug," Keelin whispered.

Flynn pulled her into his arms, and she felt the heat spread. Keelin began to recite nursery rhymes in her head to keep from devouring his mouth. Flynn wore no shirt and his cargo shorts hung low on a torso that was tanned from the sun, and as chiseled as the cliffs that surrounded him. Keelin wanted to run her tongue down the little curve of muscle that dipped into his shorts. What did they call that area on a man anyway? It was so sexy.

Nursery rhymes, Keelin reminded herself, and eased slowly away.

Flynn's breath puffed out in small huffs. His blue eyes bored into hers. There was a question and a demand there.

"I can't. I just, I can't." Keelin wasn't sure what question she was answering.

"Let me know when you figure it out," Flynn said quietly.

Keelin was scared she had already figured it out but wasn't sure if she was leaving one current to be swept away in another.

Flynn lifted the motor and let the boat bump gently against the shore. He hopped out easily and stood in the water, offering his arms to her.

Keelin took the coward's way out and dove into the water. She needed a moment to cool off. Surfacing, she caught his wolfish grin. He knew she was avoiding him.

Nose in the air, she walked to the shore, pulling her gear with her. Flynn followed, tugging the boat partially up onto the sand.

The puppy yipped hysterically and Keelin ran over to Ronan, glad for the excuse to ignore Flynn.

"Shh, it's okay. I'm okay. Shh, good boy, Ronan." He wiggled in her lap, yipping and barking. Flynn walked over to them and smiled down at the puppy.

"Ronan, huh?"

"Yes, my little warrior. Um, thank you for him." Keelin wanted to avoid what his note had said. She thought of Margaret and how she had always drilled proper manners into her. "Um, also, you're right. You didn't take advantage of me. I shouldn't have said that." Keelin blushed and looked at her feet.

"Thank you." Flynn bent over and scratched Ronan under his chin. The puppy dissolved in wriggles on the sand and Flynn laughed. Keelin knew how the puppy felt; she was a puddle in Flynn's hands as well.

Sensing her thoughts, Flynn looked up at her from under heavy-lidded eyes. Keelin took a deep breath. Whoa, boy. A shirtless man, cut like a god, playing with a puppy on an empty beach. She was toast.

"Um, have you ever seen gold in the water? Like do you swim here?" Keelin babbled out. So much for being a professional, she thought. She sounded like a middle-school girl.

"Gold? What do you mean? Are you talking about rumors of the chalice?" Flynn frowned at her.

"I don't know. It was just so confusing. I kept seeing like this flash of gold or something underwater, which is how I ended up way further out than I should have been. I just couldn't place it and it wasn't a fish or something. It was the strangest thing."

"Ahh, yes, I've heard of this before. Are you sure you haven't been listening to the local lore?" Flynn asked.

"No, what do you mean?"

"Well, supposedly, the cove will lead you out of it if it feels like you are trying to uncover something it doesn't want to share. Like the chalice. Most people won't come here, as everyone who has ulterior motives has been injured or killed."

"No! Do you really believe that?"

"Yes. What were your motives for coming here today?" Flynn stared at her. Through her.

Keelin dug her toe into the sand and didn't meet his eyes.

"Well, you know, I'm doing my thesis, was just wanting to study the ocean life and see the lay of the land so to speak. Nothing crazy."

"Hmm. Well it seems as though the cove disagrees." He just looked at her patiently.

Keelin felt like a child being chastised.

"Okay, maybe I thought I might be able to find the chalice. Or figure out what that blue light was." She stopped talking. She could have slapped herself for bringing up the blue light and last night. They both knew when the cove had lit up and what they had been doing at the time.

A slow smile spread across Flynn's face.

"Maybe we need to do some research. A reenactment, perhaps?"

"Ugh, shut up. Last night was a mistake. I had a bit too much to drink and haven't dated anyone in a while. That's all it was and nothing more. Can we just forget about it and be, like, friends or neighbors or whatever? Honestly, you aren't even my type."

Flynn's smile widened and Keelin huffed out a breath. Enough of this. She needed to get away from him. She reached over and began stuffing her snorkel stuff in her bag and moved to stand up. Flynn reacted quickly. He jerked her to her feet and pulled her to him, crushing her mouth under his. Keelin whimpered. His arms closed around her, rock hard, imprisoning her against his chest. Her hands fell to her sides and her bag dropped. Flynn caressed her with his mouth, whisper-soft in his kisses as he dipped and dived, gently sucking on her lower lip. Keelin moaned at the contrast of his strong arms forcing her to be still and the gentleness of his kiss. Helpless not to respond, she opened her mouth and kissed him back.

She stumbled back as his arms suddenly released her. Flynn steadied her with his hands on her shoulders. He touched his finger to her lips, caressing their shape, and tucked her hair behind her ear.

"Not your type, huh?" Flynn stared pointedly down at her breasts – her nipples puckered against her wetsuit – and ran a hand down her side.

"Get some rest, Keelin." Flynn reached down and patted Ronan on the head and strolled away whistling. Cursing him, Keelin grabbed her bag and Ronan and made a break for the path. She'd had enough of both Flynn and the cove today.

Keelin trudged across the fields with Ronan loping alongside her. She could see Fiona waving to her from the garden in front of the house. She cut a path straight for the old woman. She kept quiet as Fiona bent and pet Ronan, who dissolved in wriggles at her feet. Finally, Fiona straightened and met Keelin's eyes.

"Tell me about the gold," Keelin said.

Chapter Twelve

FIONA'S SHOULDERS TENSED and she sighed as she reached out to touch Keelin's arm. Concern flitted through her eyes as she took in the stress on Keelin's face. Without saying a word, she gestured for Keelin to come inside. Briskly, Fiona walked over to a small cupboard and pulled out a worn book, and a bottle of whiskey. She poured a healthy amount of whiskey in cairn glasses and gestured for Keelin to come sit with her in the alcove, where the window was thrown open to encourage the sea breezes.

Keelin sat down and Ronan hopped into her lap. She stroked Ronan's soft ears and felt comfort seep through her. There was something soothing about having an animal curled in her lap, and she hugged him closer.

"Slàinte." Fiona issued the standard Irish cheer and toasted Keelin. They both sipped their whiskey silently. Finally, Fiona spoke.

"What happened today? Actually, I should ask what happened last night as well." Fiona met Keelin's eyes. There was steel in them.

Keelin gulped. "Um, okay, last night was stupid. I shouldn't have gone down to the cove. I know that I was being unsafe but I wasn't thinking clearly after a few ciders. It was just so confusing to me that the moonlight wouldn't shine in the cove. I was stupid though. I ran right down and scooped up a handful of water. It happened so quickly." Keelin shuddered.

"What did?" Fiona asked carefully.

"The wave. It slammed me immediately and took me under. I can't believe the force of it. There were no waves when I went down." Keelin shook her head.

Fiona nodded and stared down at her glass. "Flynn saved you last night, didn't he?"

"He did. And today. I don't even know how he always manages to be there. I guess that I should be grateful," Keelin said grumpily.

Fiona laughed. "Tell me about today."

"I went down to the cove to snorkel and I wanted to just get a lay of the land, start mapping the coral formations, and look at the variety of species in the water. I did what you said for protection." Keelin explained what she did for the ritual, her initial impression of the water, and how she quickly got dragged out to sea. She downplayed Flynn's rescue so as not to worry the older woman.

Fiona eyed her closely.

"It had to have been a bigger deal than you are saying as there is an exceptionally strong current outside the cove. Most people don't come back from that. You are very lucky that Flynn was there."

"Grr. I know, I know." Keelin knew she sounded like a whiny child.

Fiona smiled.

"Get your knickers in a bundle, does he?"

Keelin choked on her sip of whiskey and broke into a coughing fit.

"Grandma!"

"What? I was a young woman once. I wasn't unaffected by strong muscles and chiseled jawbones, you know. How do you think I fell in love with your grandfather?" Fiona winked and Keelin laughed.

"What do you plan to do about him?" Fiona asked casually.

"I don't know. He scares the shit out of me to be honest."

"Even better," Fiona said.

"I don't want to talk about Flynn. Tell me about the gold that I thought I saw. What happened today?" Keelin asked. She was uncomfortable discussing Flynn. She already spent too much time thinking about him.

Fiona picked up the small book she had pulled out earlier. She began paging through it silently, nodding a few times, and then closed it.

"This book has been passed down from Grace O'Malley's daughter. She speaks of her mother in here as well as the cove. One of her mother's greatest wishes was to be left in peace as she chose her final resting place to be the cove. This is the reason we do the protection ritual and bring offerings. It is sacred water."

"But I did it! I did the ritual and brought offerings." Keelin huffed out an angry breath.

"Then your purposes for being there were impure."

Keelin immediately flashed to Flynn and his strong hands wrenching an orgasm from her. She flushed.

Fiona's eyes crinkled at the corners. "Impure as in you wanted something from the cove. Why did you go there today?"

"I told you, to work on my studies."

"You're lying." Fiona sipped her whiskey calmly.

Keelin stopped. Why had she gone there today? Of course it was for her studies, she thought. Liar, liar, her brain whispered to her. She looked into Fiona's knowing eyes.

"I wanted to find the chalice. What a huge accomplishment it would be for my beginning career and for Ireland's National Museum!" Keelin blurted it out and then stared down at her hands.

Fiona reached over and patted Keelin's hand.

"You're lucky. It's a hard lesson to learn that most don't live through. I'll be forever thankful that Flynn was there today. I'll invite him over for dinner this week to thank him." Fiona smiled.

Keelin started to protest and then stopped. Margaret had bred manners into her and she knew that a thank you would be polite. She was grateful that Fiona didn't make a bigger deal of her reasons behind going to the cove today. She was embarrassed to realize how selfish she had been in her goals. In doing so, she had disrupted sacred waters.

"Plus he gave you this sweet puppy. Does this mean that you are staying then?" Fiona asked, casually cleaning up their glasses and putting the book away.

Startled, Keelin looked up at Fiona. She certainly knew how to cut to the quick of things.

"I, um, well. Yes, I was considering extending my stay indefinitely if you didn't mind. I think it is time to take myself more seriously. I mean, you know, this healing stuff." Keelin flushed.

"Ah, yes." Fiona nodded and smiled.

"I think a part of me will die if I don't," Keelin blurted out.

"That is the way of power. Most people are intuitive, you know, though most don't have the type of gifts that you and I have. However, a gift of power, denied repeatedly, dims, and eventually one can no longer hear it or feel it. It is no longer your reality. In denying it, a piece of you *will* die."

Keelin had suspected as much. She thought again of life in Boston. Finish school, marry a nice young man, start a family…and on into oblivion. There was no punch, no spice in Boston. Grace's Cove was magic and so was she. It was time to accept and harness it. Light filled her and she smiled. Her gut sang and she knew her intuition was right. She was home. Her mother was going to lose it.

"I'll be glad to have the company. It gets lonely here," Fiona said.

"I'll be here, Grandma. You have me now."

Chapter Thirteen

THE NEXT DAY dawned with a gentle breeze. The sun kissed the shoreline as Ronan yipped to go outside. Keelin struggled awake from a night of steamy dreams about Flynn. That man was going to drive her crazy. Ronan whined at the foot of her bed.

"Okay, let's go outside."

She pulled a loose sweatshirt on over her tank and sleep shorts and padded outside, enjoying the sunshine and stunning view while Ronan did his business. She shielded her eyes against the sun and looked up to the ridgeline. Flynn's dog watched her. She waved and she could have sworn the dog damn near waved back as it lifted its paw.

"I must be losing it."

Too much talk of power and magic was making her a little nuts. She laughed as she imagined what Margaret would make of all this. She made a note to call her mother later that day.

Ronan let out a warning growl, his hair on end. Fiona approached from the path and, recognizing her scent, he let out happy barks and raced to meet her, upending himself and rolling over as he got to her. She laughed like a girl and ruffled his ears. Ronan was good for them both, Keelin thought.

"Where were you?" Keelin asked.

"I was gathering some special herbs that were ready to harvest. I have a tincture that I am making for Mrs. Sullivan in the village. Her arthritis is acting up."

Keelin realized that she had been so focused on her own stuff that she hadn't thought to ask Fiona about her "practice."

"Do you do this a lot? Provide remedies for people on a regular basis? I got the impression that people only came to you in serious times of need."

Fiona stretched her lower back and looked out at the water before answering.

"It depends. Some people fear me. They make the sign of the cross as I pass, as though I was something evil and not a God-fearing Christian such as themselves. Little do they know that there is more than just God out there and they need to open their minds. However, there are plenty of people that see me for what I am – a healer. Most assume that is through potions, tinctures, and herbal ointments that I create. Some suspect magic. Very few have seen the physical effects of what I am able to do with my hands. Those that have say nothing, as it is usually done only in the direst of circumstances. Only when people are pushed to the threshold of pain for themselves or a loved one are they willing to suspend their beliefs on what works. Only then will they believe that healing can come in many ways not prescribed by modern medicine."

"What do you say to people when they see you heal?"

"Nothing. I'm not required to explain myself, nor do I think I could accurately do so. I can no more tell you why I have this gift than I can tell you how many stars in the sky there are."

Keelin supposed it made sense. From a scientific standpoint, there was no logical explanation for healing through touch. The closest thing she could think of was massage or acupuncture, but to close wounds or to pull sickness from a body? That was a whole different realm. She wondered if studies had been done on this.

Keelin looked down at her hands. Small, with rounded nails cut short, and no nail polish, they hid the power they held. Was it time to step into her own and accept that she would never be normal?

"I want to learn. All of it. I'll start taking my lessons seriously. On one condition."

Fiona turned and looked at her, a smile hovering on her lips.

"I want you to take me into the cove. I promise that I won't take anything out of the cove. But I need to see it. I need to know what is in there. Something is pulling me there."

Fiona's hands continued to adeptly tie the bundles of herbs she had picked. She was silent for a long moment as Ronan raced across the yard, chasing a butterfly. The cove spread out before them. It beckoned to Keelin.

"Yes. I can no more keep you from the water than you can keep me from the hills. It's in your blood. We'll begin today."

Satisfied, Keelin called for Ronan. They both had some growing up to do.

Fiona packed a bag lunch for the both of them. She gathered the worn leather book, various jars, several crystals, and shears to harvest herbs. Keelin packed her snorkeling gear and put together a bag of toys and water for Ronan. Fiona surprised her when she pulled out old, yet serviceable, snorkel equipment.

"You dive?" Keelin asked.

"Of course, my dear. You can't live on the water and not know the water."

Impressed, Keelin picked up Fiona's gear and carried both as they made their way to the edge of the cliffs. It was one of those perfect summer days. The sun warmed the Kerry green of the grass that carpeted the rolling hills behind them, and the stark edges of the cliffs hugged the gentle waters of the cove, and the waves lapped invitingly on the empty sand beach. Keelin inhaled the sea air, a deep breath that she dragged into her core, and exhaled, allowing the tension to fade from her. Purity of purpose, she thought.

They carefully picked their way down the path on the ledge, Ronan running excitedly ahead of them.

"Will Ronan be harmed here?" Keelin asked.

"Most likely not. A dog's purpose is to love life and to serve its master. They care little for harming the cove. The cove knows that," Fiona said.

They reached the base and stopped. Fiona pulled out several small crystals in varying shapes and colors. She held them in her hand and drew a circle in the sand around them.

"Oh sacredest of sacred waters, we come to you today to learn and grow. Anything we take from here will be for the purest form of healing and nothing more. We pay our due respects by offering you these stones. We ask that our angels serve as protection as we enter these sacred waters in the most humble of manners." Fiona handed Keelin some crystals and they gently threw them into the waters of the cove.

"That should be good. Let's get Ronan set up in a spot."

Fiona and Keelin spent the afternoon snorkeling in the waters of the cove. Fiona knew all of the nooks and crannies and soon Keelin found herself immersed in the varying coral formations that lined the length of the cove.

As the shadows began to deepen, Keelin and Fiona sat on the beach, Ronan running in circles around them. Fiona laid out their finds for the day. Before them lay piles of rocks, corals, and crystals, some of which Keelin couldn't classify. There was a pile of kelp, seaweed, sea urchins, and mussels. Sand and deep clay lay damply in several large mason jars. A pile of moss scraped from the rocks further out in the cove lay out, drying in the sun. Fiona spent time explaining the various uses for the seaweed, the mosses, and how different crystals used different healing energies. Keelin made notes in her book and tried to look at it like a chemistry class. She was worried though. She'd never been a good cook and a lot of this sounded like recipes. What if she screwed it up and hurt someone?

Fiona seemed to read her mind, and laughed.

"Practice. You'll learn all of this. And, ultimately, it is learning to trust your own intuition. Your own power will tell you if you are doing something wrong or if you are using the wrong potion or wrong ingredient. It is very different than following recipes to a T. There is no exact science with this. These are the ingredients. Your potions and ointments will be different than mine. Yours will work with you better than they will with me. You just have to trust in yourself."

"What if I screw it up? What if I hurt someone?" Keelin blurted out.

"We all make mistakes. How do you think a doctor feels when they first start out? You have to learn to listen to yourself and believe in your own power. Start there. Start small. It will build."

As the sun began to dip low, they gathered their supplies and turned to head home. Keelin caught a faint blue glow in the cove.

"There! See, look, look!" She grabbed Fiona and turned her just as the light faded.

"You've seen it!" Fiona said.

"Yes, what is it? I can't figure it out."

"I've been researching for years. The best that I can piece together is that the cove will light up for its own. I also know that it glows in the presence of love."

Keelin blushed as her thoughts flashed to Flynn sending her over the edge the other night. The cove had definitely glowed blue then. But, love? No way. She barely knew this enigmatic Flynn. Which, she reminded herself, was why she shouldn't be kissing him, let alone letting him underneath her clothes.

As they approached the cottage, Ronan growled and let out some warning barks. A late-model sedan was parked in front and Keelin recognized blond Shane from the pub the other night.

"Hmpf," Fiona said as she nodded to him and sailed past him inside.

"Um, sorry about that. She's had a long day," Keelin said. Shane walked around the car as Ronan stood in front of Keelin, barking at Shane. He was dressed in business clothes today, his tie pulled loose and his top button open. His white shirt was crisp and tucked into Irish-wool pants. He bent over to let Ronan smell his hand. Ronan approached him and gave his hand a tentative lick, then backed up and sat on Keelin's feet.

Shane grinned down at him and then looked Keelin up and down. She knew she was mussed and sandy, and blushed a bit. Her tank top clung to her wetsuit and her shorts had sand on them.

"Where'd this little guy come from?" he asked.

"Um, a gift from a friend." Keelin wasn't sure why she didn't say it was from Flynn.

"Looks like one of Flynn's. He has some of the best dogs in the country. You're lucky to have one."

Keelin hadn't know that Flynn bred dogs. Chalk it up to another thing she didn't know about the man. She preferred to think of him as a surly, uncommunicative fisherman. The picture of him lovingly nursing a mama dog flashed into her mind and she softened a bit.

"Yes, he is quite a sweetheart. So, what brings you here today?" Keelin brushed sand from her arm and tried to stop herself from peeling her tank top from her suit. She felt like she was on display.

"I stopped to see if I could take you to dinner." Shane stared at her very directly, his intentions clear.

"Me? What about..." Keelin stopped. She was about to say, "What about Cait," yet she had no idea what their relationship was, nor was it any of her business. It wasn't like she had heard from Cait since she had been here either. Still, she knew small towns and didn't want to start the gossip mill running. That being said, she was certain Flynn would hear of it. That decided it for her.

"Sure, I would love to go to dinner. But! Just as friends," Keelin said sternly.

Shane's smiled broadened. "Sure, friends it is. I'll wait while you change."

"Okay, I need a little time to shower."

"That's fine, I'll enjoy the sunset and talk to Ronan."

Keelin dropped her gear inside and went to shower, passing Fiona muttering at the kitchen counter.

"I'm going to dinner with Shane. I'm not sure when I will be back. Do you need anything from the village?"

"No. And you be careful with that man."

Keelin stopped at her doorway. "What is your problem with him? You sailed right past him and barely said a word. Yet you treat Flynn like he's God. What's the deal?" Keelin hissed at her, hoping her voice didn't carry.

"He's not for you," Fiona said enigmatically, and turned back to knead her bread. Conversation was over, apparently. Keelin threw up her hands and went to shower.

In deference to the warm evening, Keelin pulled her hair back and let it flow down her shoulders, curling mildly with the sea air. She pulled on a navy blue linen sundress that complemented her hair color and deep brown eyes, and put on some thin silver necklaces. She pulled out a flat pair of strappy silver sandals and a small bag. The sun had touched her skin with color so a little lip gloss and mascara was all she needed. It would be nice to go out and learn more about the town.

Keelin left her room and stopped by Fiona's chair.

"I told him it was just as friends. Just so you know."

"Mmhmm. I know what you're doing. Be careful the games you play."

"Oh, stop. This isn't the 1900s. Girls can have guys as friends, you know. I have several in Boston," Keelin said definitively.

Fiona nodded and didn't say anything. Sighing, Keelin picked up her purse and stroked Ronan under his chin. She let herself out of the cottage and caught a glimpse of movement up on the ridgeline. She could have sworn she saw the shadow of a man but it could have been a sheep for all she knew. Or cared. Shane straightened from his perch on the front bumper of his car and whistled. Keelin laughed.

"Oh, stop."

"I'm telling you, Keelin O'Brien, you are a knockout."

Keelin blushed but enjoyed the compliment. Though she knew the Irish were famous for their charm, it was still nice to get compliments. It was so different in the States. She caught herself giggling and realized she would have to be careful around Shane. His good ol' boy routine housed a wolfish interior. Laying low on the liquor tonight would be smart.

Shane took the sea route into the village and they laughed and talked of local gossip as the sun set and the color of the water deepened. The breeze fluttered her hair as it dried and Keelin relaxed into the seat. It was a beautiful night.

Shane took her to a local seafood joint right on the water. It was a small place, painted a cheerful red, with its brown shutters thrown open to catch the sea breezes. The scents of seafood soaked in butter made her mouth water.

They were shown to a small table in the corner. A chunky candle sputtered in a mason jar layered with sand and seashells. Sea nets hung around the restaurant, framing walls with photos of the water. It was charming in its simplicity.

"I know it doesn't look like much but the food here is first class," Shane said as he put his napkin in his lap and pulled out the wine list. "Would you like some wine?"

"Sure, I'll have a glass." Keelin made a point of reminding herself that this would be her only glass of the night. She saw a few waitresses whispering to each other in the corner and looking curiously at them. She groaned.

"I think we are stirring up gossip already," Keelin said.

"Does that bother you?" Shane said as he openly assessed her. Keelin looked at him. It was clear his intentions hadn't changed.

"Hey, I said just as friends," Keelin reminded him.

"Friends go to lunch or on a walk. A candlelit dinner says more. I think you are sending mixed signals, Ms. Keelin," Shane said.

"Hey, that's not fair. I told you this was just as friends." His intentness was beginning to irritate her.

"I think you knew exactly what you were doing when you went to dinner with me. The question I wonder: is it because you are attracted to me or is it because you are using me to send a message to a certain gentleman who gave you a puppy?" Shane's directness shocked her.

Never one to back down, Keelin stared right back at him. She opened her mouth to speak but the waitress interrupted her.

"Good evening, then. Can I get you something to drink? A pint, perhaps?" The girl's eyes shone bright with interest.

"We'll have a bottle of the local chardonnay." Shane ordered for them quickly and sent the waitress on her way.

"Listen, pal. You don't know me." Keelin felt her emotions building.

"No, but I'd like to." Shane grinned wolfishly at her.

Keelin thought she would smack him. And then she caught something else in his eyes. Loneliness glinted there. Remembering Fiona's instruction to listen to her intuition, she reached out and grabbed Shane's hand and let herself read him. Feelings assaulted her. Sadness, attraction, loneliness, and a deeper layer of kindness. Taking her hand off of his, she looked at him quietly.

"So this is all an act." Keelin stated matter-of-factly.

"What are you talking about?" Shane was flustered for the first time since she had met him.

"This. This whole thing. Your pretend attraction to me. The rich, successful guy sweeping women off their feet. The wolfish grin. All of this. That's not really you. You're a nice guy," Keelin said.

Shane sighed. He pulled at his necktie and accepted the wine from the waitress. He didn't say anything else as they both ordered the local mussels. He took a long drink of his wine and stared out at the sea before answering.

"First, I *am* attracted to you. You're a knockout. Those curves, lips made for nibbling on, and all that hair. I'd love to see it spread across my sheets."

Heat burned through Keelin. So, she wasn't totally immune to him after all. Shane had his own seduction, it seemed.

"That being said, I know you aren't attracted to me. It was just that you are new in town, and, and, well you're right. I'm lonely. It isn't easy being in the position I am in. Most people prefer not to get too close to me as I can be the one who will evict them or close their business down if they don't make rent. I love being successful, but it is lonely at the top."

Keelin gave him her first unguarded smile of the night.

"See, this is good stuff. I think we can be friends after all. Let's talk."

Shane stared at her and a delighted laugh barked out of his mouth. Once the tension eased a bit, Keelin was surprised to find that they had much to talk about and the evening wore on as they learned more about each other's families, mutual likes, and the local gossip.

"So, what are you going to do about your brother and sister?" Shane asked over dessert.

"I don't know. I haven't been into town much. Just, um, been building my relationship with my grandma. I don't really know how to handle this situation with my brother and sister."

"I admire both your sister and brother, though they seem like they are not even related to each other. Colin is uptight and very serious. He is very devoted to his wife though and his young son. Aislinn on the other hand is a dreamer. Her artwork is stunning."

"Wait, I have a nephew?" Keelin took a deep gulp of her wine. She laughed a little. Of course she had a nephew, why wouldn't she have? She shook her head.

"Yes, Finnegan. He's a delightful child. Colin is protective of him. You might meet some resistance there," Shane said frankly.

"I think that I may start with my sister. She sounds like the easier going of the two. I'll talk to Fiona about it and maybe I'll stop by her store. I've been meaning to stop in and have a pint with Cait anyway." Keelin watched Shane closely. He lifted his chin stubbornly and didn't say anything as he signed the check.

Keelin sighed. "Come on! Aren't you going to tell me what is going on with you two? If you and I are going to be friends and all?" she prodded.

"Are you going to tell me what's going on with you and Flynn?" Shane retaliated.

Shit, Keelin thought. She wasn't prepared to think about that herself let alone hash it out with someone else.

"Fine. I won't ask you about Cait. On one condition. Tell me everything you know about Flynn."

Shane smiled as he walked her to the car, his hand on the small of her back. He opened the door and leaned in to brush her hair back as she got in the car. She looked at him questioningly.

"Just giving the servers something to gossip about. Flynn owns this restaurant."

Keelin groaned. Leave it to Shane to let this little detail slide until the end of the night. He got in the car and she punched him in the shoulder.

"Ow! What was that for!" Shane winced.

"You knew this was Flynn's restaurant and you said nothing? You jerk!"

"Oh, stop. You wanted to make him jealous or you wouldn't have gone out with me. And what better place to do it in than his own restaurant?" Shane raised his eyebrows at Keelin.

Keelin knew he was right. She didn't always like to admit to this baser part of herself. But she did want to make a point that Flynn wasn't the only thing on her mind. Though he had played a predominant part in her dreams as of late.

"Tell me about him."

Shane started the car and pointed it up towards the longer route home. This was a drive Keelin hadn't taken yet and she watched the lights slice over the hedges as they climbed higher into the hills.

"Flynn is a little bit of an outcast. He likes to keep to himself, yet he is very popular in town. He does a little bit of everything. A fisherman at heart, he also owns acres of land that head far up into the hills. He has a strong affinity for animals and has spent years cultivating the best Irish setters in the country. That little pup of yours was more than just a gift; it most likely cost a thousand Euros."

Keelin let out a shocked sound. She had known that Ronan was important but she thought it was more because Flynn was forcing her to make a choice on staying. She hadn't stopped to consider the cost of the dog, and the sheer enormity of such a gift hit her. Was Flynn wooing her? She began to feel a little lousy about her evening with Shane. What kind of message was that to Flynn? Even though he was bad-tempered, he had saved her several times –she didn't want to think how many times – and had given her the expensive gift of Ronan. Keelin realized that she may have been missing a few signals along the way. But damn, that man got her Irish up.

"What about his family?" she asked.

"Both his parents have passed on. His father was a fisherman and he often fished with your father. His mother was an artist and her work was well renowned. Flynn moved to their house when they both died and has been living there ever since. Aside from me, he is one of the most successful men in the village. Don't let his rugged farm-boy looks fool you; that man is rich as can be. That restaurant you just ate in? He owns fifteen of them up the coast of Ireland. Each unique, each charming, and each packed, standing room only, every night of the week. His fresh catch of the day is renowned and the mussels he pulls from Grace's Cove are famous. No other restaurant is able to claim their mussels come from there. Nobody else dares to go there. Flynn is a master in his own right."

Keelin was floored by this information. Flynn was rich? Here she thought he was a poor fisherman making his living by his daily catch. She would need to reevaluate her opinion of him from poor farmer/fisherman to cunning businessman. For some reason, it made her angry. She felt like he had misrepresented himself to her and it didn't sit well with her.

"He never said a word." Keelin stared into the dark as the car climbed higher into the hills.

"He wouldn't. Flynn doesn't talk about money." Shane crested over a ridge and they looked down at the lights of a large ranch house, triple the size of Fiona's, that spread out overlooking the hills. Several stables were lit and clustered closely to the house. Keelin could see horses being led in from the pasture and several dogs running around. Floodlights illuminated the spread and it was neat, clean, and beautifully appointed. A variety of different sized boats were on trailers tucked behind the stables.

"Flynn's?" Keelin asked.

"Flynn's," Shane said. He wound the car down the hills towards Fiona's house and Flynn's spread disappeared from view. Keelin couldn't believe how much he oversaw. That man seemed to be everywhere at once and he had so much responsibility. She was amazed to find her attraction growing. This was the type of man Margaret would approve of. It didn't make sense.

Shane pulled quietly into the drive and cut the lights. He leaned back and turned his head towards hers. "Wanna make out?"

Keelin smacked him on the shoulder again.

"Ow, I had to try. I mean, we might as well see if there is anything between us then."

Snaking his hand out, he slipped his arm behind her and dove in for a kiss. Shocked, Keelin didn't move for a second. She let his mouth move over hers, testing, kissing gently. She tried it out for a second and was relieved to feel nothing. Taking a deep breath, she punched him in the gut.

"Oough! Youch. You've got a nasty punch." Shane doubled over and looked at her, deeply wounded.

"Stop it. You know you didn't feel anything anymore than I did."

Shane sighed. "You're right. I wanted to though. I really would like to run my hands down your curves. Sure I can't change your mind?" He leered at her. This time she saw it for what it was and laughed at him. Leaning over, she gave him a hug and thanked him for dinner.

She closed the door and peered in the window. "Go take a cold shower."

He laughed and waved, pulling out of the drive carefully. Keelin could hear Ronan's yips inside. She let herself in and saw a note on the table. "The O'Briens' boy is ill, I'm not sure when I will be home." Feeling guilty for not being there to help Fiona out, Keelin put her purse down and knelt to pet Ronan. The puppy writhed in ecstasy and she laughed down at him.

"I should've called you something more suiting a fancy king that you are." He tumbled over and lay with his paws up, grinning at her endearingly. "Come on, let's take you out for a walk."

Keelin slipped her sandals off but kept her dress on. They wouldn't go far. She opened the door and let an ecstatic Ronan race out into the darkness.

"Hey, come back here. Shit." Keelin scrambled for the flashlight by the door and walked out into the fields. As she moved away from the house, the darkness felt overpowering. The house glowed against the hills, and the half moon offered a little light. She could barely see Ronan as he bounded through the fields away from the house.

"Hey, Ronan! Get back here." She half-laughed as she chased him over the ridge and stopped short.

Ronan ran in circles around Flynn's dog. She patiently licked the puppy's face as he jumped on her.

Flynn stood behind his dog, a lantern in his hand. The flames shot warm light across his face, but his eyes were in darkness. She swore they stared into her soul. Liquid heat slipped low in her belly. He didn't even have to touch her to get a response, Keelin thought, as she remembered how Shane's kiss evoked no response in her.

"Have a nice dinner, Keelin?" Flynn's words were like silk against her skin.

"Um, yes. I just learned that the restaurant we ate at is yours. Dinner was lovely." Keelin wanted to ask him why he hadn't told her that he owned restaurants. Probably because half of the time they weren't talking, she reminded herself.

Flynn walked towards her, bent down, and put the lantern on the ground. It cast a low circle of light around them. Keelin's breath slowed. Flynn moved forward until

131

he was inches away from her. An arc of energy zipped between them and Keelin's skin felt sensitized. Her breaths came out in shallow puffs as she looked up at him.

"Do you like Shane? Do you like another man's lips on yours? Is this what you do in Boston?" Flynn said tersely.

He was angry. Keelin could feel it radiating off him. She gulped and looked at his chest and then dragged her eyes upwards, over his heavenly mouth, and into those devastatingly blue eyes. Her lips suddenly dry, she licked them before answering.

"I, no. I don't. I'm not like that. I told Shane it was just as friends."

"Do you let all your friends kiss you like that, Keelin?" Flynn's voice was accusatory.

Keelin lost it. She smacked him lightly in the chest and he stumbled back a foot, surprised.

"Hey, it's not like you are showing up at my door and asking me to dinner. I have every right to do what I want. So stop with this, whatever this is," she fumed at him.

"Damn, you are the most infuriating woman." Flynn grabbed her and crushed his lips to hers. She kicked him in the shin and he swore, backing up a step.

"Hands off." Keelin's words mocked her body, which screamed "Hands on!" She wanted to run her tongue all over him and have him make her scream. Focus, she thought. Focus. Shane had taught her one thing tonight. This was a small town and gossips were everywhere. If she let Flynn kiss her all over the hills, somehow someone would see and her reputation in town would be ruined. She hadn't even had time to make friends yet, and she was far from wanting to be labeled as easy girl in town who let two different men kiss her in a night.

"Listen up, buddy, I'm not that kind of girl. You think you can just get everything you want for free? Well you can't." Her mind screamed at her, "liar, liar, pants on fire." She wanted to rip her sundress off and dance naked in the moonlight with him. There was something so pagan about the lantern light, the moon, and the waves crashing. Oh yeah, she could all but feel it.

Flynn ran his hands through his hair and then cocked them on his hips, staring her down.

"I can see your nipples through your dress. You want me."

"Stop it. Don't talk to me like that. If you want to be with me than you can take me on a date," Keelin fumed at him.

"So it's a date you want, Miss Keelin? Then it's a date you'll get, but I'll be getting a down payment on that first."

Flynn reached out and wound his hand through her hair. He gently tugged until she stepped forward, closing the gap between them. Her breasts brushed his muscled chest, and Keelin caught her breath. Flynn tugged her hair down until she was forced to look up at him. Flynn leaned down and laid a whisper of a kiss on her lips. Once, twice, a third time, gently kissing her, his hand holding her hair, not touching her elsewhere. Her hands hung suspended at her sides, her body locked to his, as he softly teased her with his mouth. She moaned. He smiled and stepped back. Keelin stumbled a bit.

Flynn steadied her and said, "Clear your evening this Saturday. It's a full moon. I'll take you on my boat." He whistled for his dog and, picking up his lantern, walked into the night.

Keelin shouted after him, "Oh, sure. Yes, I'd love to. Thanks for asking so nicely!" She could hear his chuckle float over the dark air.

Cursing him, and her clearly wanton ways, she picked the whimpering Ronan up and headed back to the cottage.

Chapter Fourteen

THE PHONE STARTLED Keelin and she shot up in bed. The gray light of dawn touched the windows. Keelin reached for her cell phone before she realized it was the house phone. She jerked up and whipped the covers off of the bed, and rushed out into the main room. Fiona was nowhere to be seen. Keelin fumbled with the receiver as Ronan ran excitedly after her, nipping at her heels.

"Ronan, stop! Hello?" Keelin tucked her hair behind her ear and blinked the fuzzies out of her eyes after another angsty night of x-rated dreams featuring Flynn, with a surprise appearance by Shane. She was turning into a wanton. Or something. This town was making her nuts.

"Keelin, it's Fiona."

"Grandma, didn't you come home?" Keelin was surprised. She realized that she hadn't seen her car last night after all. She fell asleep so quickly after returning to the house that she hadn't heard if Fiona had come in.

"No, Finnegan is deathly ill. This is beyond what I can handle on my own. I need you."

"Grandma. I don't know what to do! What if I make it worse?" Keelin paced, flinging her hand out as she spoke.

"Keelin. I need you. I am failing. I can only take so much of this in myself. He's only seven. He deserves a chance at life."

Keelin realized she was letting her insecurities get in the way of saving a life.

"Okay, what do you need me to bring?" Keelin grabbed a pencil and wrote down all of the supplies that Fiona needed. She looked down at Ronan. She didn't know how long she would be gone. She popped the door open and whistled long and low. Moments later, Flynn's dog popped over the ridge. If she had the man's phone number like modern people she would just call him, she thought sarcastically. Instead, she tied a brief note to Ronan's collar and sent him up to Flynn's dog. They raced together over the ridgeline and she hoped that Ronan would be safe. Gathering her supplies, she slipped on jeans, a simple t-shirt, and the crystal necklace that Fiona had given her. The necklace was warm against her breast and seemed to hum with energy. Good, she thought. I can use any energy that will help me. She had no idea what she was about to walk into.

Keelin hopped into her ragged truck and made her way into the village, following her hastily scrawled directions.

She pulled up at a small house as Cait came out of the front door, a haggard look on her face. Seeing Keelin, she glared and stomped off.

"Cait! Wait, I want to talk to you!"

"No time to talk, I have to open the pub."

Seeing as it was fairly early in the morning hours, Keelin highly doubted that Cait needed to open the pub. Word had gotten around quickly about her date with Shane. Keelin would make it a point to go visit Cait later but for now she was needed inside.

Keelin entered the cottage. The musk of sickness hit her as she walked towards the voices in the back room. She entered a small room with a single bed tucked into a corner. The furnishings were minimal, but the linens were clean, and the coverlet had been made with care. Several people huddled over a small figure on the bed. A man turned as she walked into the room and she stopped. Keelin stared into eyes shaped like hers and flinched.

Her brother looked at her and said nothing. A small woman at his side turned and gasped. "Oh, thank you so much for coming. I don't know if Fiona can hold out much longer." She grasped Keelin's hand and pulled her past her brother, who remained silent. Fiona sat on a small chair by the bed. Her face was ashen and she held crystals in her palms as she muttered under her breath. Keelin immediately worried for her.

"Fiona. Grandma, I'm here." Keelin placed her palms on Fiona's shoulders and felt her exhaustion.

Fiona nodded, never taking her eyes off of the small boy who lay in the bed. His face was almost deathly white, a sheen of sweat across his brow, and deep gray hollows ringed his eyes. His brown hair matched his father's and when he opened his eyes, they mirrored Keelin's. This was her nephew.

"Finnegan, this is your Aunt Keelin from America. She's here to help you," Fiona said as she stroked his brow. Keelin didn't know what to say and then realized they were waiting for her to speak.

"Hi, Finnegan. So nice to finally meet you. You're looking a little down; let's get you fixed up so you can get back outside. I have a new puppy for you to meet." Keelin chattered nonsense words as her brother pulled up a chair next to the bed for her. She sat down and pulled the sack of materials onto her lap. Fiona nodded and took the sack. She moved over to the table and dumped everything out and began mixing a new broth.

Keelin turned to her. "Do you need me?" She was scared to touch Finnegan. She wasn't sure what she was dealing with yet.

"Yes. First, hold his hand and read him." Fiona asked for boiling water and poured a mixture of herbs into the bowl. Keelin leaned over Finnegan and reached for his hand. His small hand was cold in hers, and she was immediately pulled under by sensations. She could feel a deep pain, and sensed a dark residue of sorts that was attacking his nervous system. She heard Fiona tell her to pay attention to the toxin but not to remove it. Keelin forced herself to feel where the toxin was and to examine the properties of it. She tried to envision what it looked like, down to the molecular structure.

"Keelin, come here." Fiona beckoned with the small bowl.

Keelin walked over to the table and looked at the mixture Fiona had made. Fiona handed it to her.

"Smell it, taste it, and then add what is needed." Keelin almost dropped the bowl.

"I don't know what I am doing," she whispered to Fiona, standing close to her.

Fiona looked up at her. She put her hand on Keelin's necklace. Heat shot through her breast.

"Yes, you do."

Remembering Fiona's lessons on trusting her intuition and that mixing potions and healing treatments would come from within, Keelin took a deep breath and brought the image of the toxin into her head. She looked at it from all angles, felt it, and took a small sip of the healing broth her grandmother had made. Instinctively she moved towards the moss they had harvested from Grace's Cove. She added a generous portion and found herself reaching for the seaweed. She shredded fine pieces and added some finely ground silver to the mix. Thinking about taste, she asked for honey and lemon to complete the broth. Fiona nodded at her weakly.

"Go ahead, give it to him. And then use your hands. Remember what I said about directing the pain. You mustn't take it within," Fiona cautioned.

Keelin nodded. She remembered but didn't know if she knew how to do it. She just had to trust herself. She sat by Finnegan's bed and made herself comfortable, careful not to spill any of the broth from the bowl. Her hands shook as she lifted the bowl towards his small face.

"Finnegan, I have some medicine for you. If you drink this, I promise I'll bring my puppy to see you. Would you like that?" Keelin spoke softly to the sick boy.

Finnegan nodded weakly, his brown eyes huge in his face.

"Am I going to die?" he croaked out between dry lips.

"Nonsense. Just a wee bit of a fever, and this broth will help in a jiffy." Keelin prayed it was so. She could feel the amulet burning against her neck and she began to feed Finnegan the broth. As she did, ancient words rose to her lips and she recited a prayer in Gaelic. Keelin didn't know the words she spoke, yet she allowed them to come. It felt right. Slowly, Finnegan finished the broth and collapsed back on the bed, trembling.

Keelin's brother grabbed her shoulder.

"What have you done to him?" Colin pulled her off of the seat.

"Colin! No. Let her. We have nothing else. Please." His wife dragged him away. Keelin met his eyes and turned back towards Finnegan. There would be time to deal with Colin later. She sat beside Finn once again and placed her hands on his chest, near his heart. Closing her eyes, she let the sickness flood her. It was a twisted black mass. A toxin of sorts that was ravaging his small body. She visualized the broth seeping into his system, a silver stream of light and purity, and forced it to surround the black mass. Winding, dipping, and intertwining, the silver liquid slowly worked itself around the black mass and she envisioned it rolling into a ball. She focused on pulling the ball up, up, and out, and launched it out the window and into the sky, directing it towards a dying tree she saw in the yard. She heard a snap and saw a flash as a huge branch on the tree fell.

Finnegan began to cough and Keelin motioned for a bucket. The rest he could vomit out. Finnegan retched into the bucket over and over. Keelin's brother stood back, unsure of what to do. Keelin wiped Finnegan's brow as he shuddered over the bucket. Slowly, he raised his head and smiled at her. Keelin trembled as gratitude rushed through her. It was over. She ran her hands over his body but could feel no lingering sickness. Finnegan's tired eyes met hers and a flush filled his cheeks.

"Can I see the puppy now?" Keelin laughed and kissed his brow. Finnegan's mother rushed to his side, weeping as she rocked him. Keelin straightened and turned to face her brother.

"I'm sorry. I'm, I just. He's all I have." Colin brushed past Keelin and hugged Finnegan.

A wave of exhaustion hit her and she steadied herself on the table. She looked to see Fiona dozing in her chair. There was no way that Fiona would be able to drive home. Keelin wasn't certain she would be able to either.

"We need to go. Can you drive us home?" Keelin asked Colin. He broke away from Finnegan.

"Of course. I'm indebted to you," Colin said stiffly. They gathered their herbs and gently led Fiona to the car. She promptly fell asleep in the back seat and Keelin looked at her with worry.

"I, um, think she'll be okay. I've heard this happens after a serious healing," Colin said.

Keelin was surprised that he knew about Fiona but then figured she shouldn't be. It seemed to be common knowledge in the village, yet was something that wasn't openly discussed.

"Thanks for the ride; we can come get our cars in the morning," Keelin said as she rested her head against the window.

"If you give me the keys, I can have them driven out for you," Colin said stiffly.

Keelin nodded, too tired to speak.

"Thank you. I don't know what it is you do but thank you for saving my son. Your nephew. God, your nephew. I'm sorry that I haven't come to see you. I should have. I should have reached out to you. I knew you didn't know about me. I just, I've always hated you," Colin said. He kept his eyes carefully on the road.

Startled, Keelin raised her head. "Hated me? Why? What did I do?"

"I guess it wasn't you. It was the thought of you. The whole village knew that your mum was Dad's one true love. He never quite got over her and though he loved my mother, it wasn't the same. I always knew that you came first even though he never spoke of you. Aislinn and I spent our whole lives trying to live up to you. And now, here you are."

Keelin was shocked. This was too much to handle. She started to laugh. Hysterical giggles built up and she couldn't keep them quiet. Soon she was sputtering in her seat.

Colin's mouth quirked. He eyed her from the driver's seat.

"You think that's funny?"

"I, no, I, well, yes. Yes, I do. God. Oh, so stupid." Keelin wiped tears from her face. "My whole life I've always wanted a brother or sister. Anything. Siblings. And here I had them all along and they hated me! Just like normal siblings do."

Colin burst out laughing.

"Yes, I suppose you could call it a sibling rivalry of sorts. And since you saved my son, I'm likely to turn a corner and start anew. Will you come for dinner sometime this week?"

Keelin recognized an olive branch when she saw it. Eager for the connection, and the family, she reached out and touched his arm.

"Of course; I have to bring Ronan to meet Finnegan."

Colin smiled. They had reached the cottage and they woke up a gently snoring Fiona and brought her to her bed.

"It's okay, I can take it from here." Colin nodded and, giving her an awkward hug, said he would call her this week.

Keelin stripped Fiona down and tucked her in. She ran her hands over Fiona's forehead and down to her chest. Closing her eyes, she felt for the sickness. She sensed an exhaustion that mirrored her own but nothing so serious that it would harm Fiona for long. Satisfied, Keelin pulled the sheets over her and left her a pitcher of water and some brown bread by the table.

Keelin was exhausted, and starving. She rustled around in the kitchen and procured a rasher of cold bacon and a blueberry scone. She wrapped it in a towel and went outside to sit by the side of the house. She needed to sit in the sun and reenergize. She leaned her back against the warm stones of the house and faced the cove. Her necklace pulsed. Keelin was too tired to think about what it meant but she looked down and could swear the sun hit the crystal at just the right angle to make it shine with a hint of blue. Blue lights everywhere, she thought, slightly delirious. Keelin polished off her food and leaned back, letting the warmth slide over her skin. She quickly dropped into sleep.

Flynn found her there, propped up against the cottage, a small smile on her face as she slept. He watched her breasts rise gently under the t-shirt she wore and the way the sun shone in the hair that curled over her shoulder. Ronan squirmed in his arms. Flynn had an irresistible urge to pick her up and carry her home with him. He wanted her in his bed. He wanted her in his home. He wanted to protect her and challenge her at the same time. He had never met someone who had so infuriated him yet enticed him at the same time. He put Ronan on the ground and let the puppy run to her, and watched as he climbed in her lap and licked her awake with kisses.

Keelin awoke with a laugh as Ronan covered her face with happy kisses.

"Hi, buddy, I was going to come get you." She shaded her eyes as a shadow fell over her and she looked up at Flynn.

"Hey, thanks for bringing him back."

"No problem. I was somewhat concerned when I saw him racing over the hills with Teagan. Thanks for tying a note to his collar. How is the little boy?"

Flynn stretched out next to her, leaned against the cottage, and bumped shoulders with her. It was comfortable, sitting here in the sun with him. She wondered how comfortable he would be if he knew just what she was. She let out a half laugh. She didn't even know what she was. But, she was learning.

"Rough morning?" Flynn asked.

"Yes, I met my brother." Keelin decided to skip over the healing stuff. She was too raw from seeing the disease zip out of Finnegan and snap a branch off the tree. Her mind couldn't wrap itself around the how and why of it and that made her nervous. She liked things that added up neatly and made sense. A secret part of her thrilled to the knowledge that she held this power. Not that it went to her head, but it was tremendously rewarding to know she could really make a difference.

"How'd that go? Um, I've heard, well. Things." Flynn cleared his throat.

"Let me guess, you've heard that he hates me? Yeah, he told me."

"He did? Wow, he's grown even surlier than he used to be."

"It's okay. I get it. Kind of. We muddled our way through it. I'm going to dinner at his house this week and maybe we can get to know each other a little. I need to go meet my sister. She's avoided me."

"Ah, Aislinn. She's an artistic soul. Quiet. Her head is in the clouds most days but her art is beautiful. I think you'll find a better reception there."

Keelin nodded. She didn't know what to say. Here she was sitting in the sun with a man that made her want to do things that were probably illegal in this country and she spoke of family that she had never known she had. Not to mention the absurdity of her morning in flexing her healing powers. She needed to go inside and take a nap before she did something stupid. Like curl up in Flynn's lap and nuzzle into his neck.

Opting for safety, Keelin stretched and stood.

"Thank you for bringing Ronan back. I really need to go lie down for a small nap and check on Fiona."

Flynn smiled up at her disarmingly. His dimples flashed and he looked almost boyish.

"Don't forget about Saturday. I'm holding you to it."
Flynn stood up and stepped close, invading her space.
Keelin took an involuntary step backwards. Flynn brushed
her cheek with his hand and whistled to Teagan. Together,
they strode across the hill, looking like an Irish painting.
The way he moved was very "Lord of the Manor."

Keelin watched him go with a small sigh. She'd think
about Saturday another time. For now, she needed to rest
and then wanted to head into the village and talk to Cait.
She hoped Colin would bring her car back soon.

Chapter Fifteen

THE SOUND OF pans clattering in the sink woke her and Keelin stretched. The light shone warm through the windows and she checked her phone. It was mid-afternoon, yet the early morning seemed like days ago. Keelin rose and followed the noises into the kitchen.

Fiona stood at the sink, carefully washing the healing dishes that she had used earlier that day. A cup of tea steamed at her side and color had returned to her cheeks. She turned and smiled at Keelin.

"I'm so proud of you. You did good by Finnegan." Fiona walked over to embrace Keelin. Keelin smiled down into the old woman's hair and let her hold her for a moment longer.

"Thank you. I truly had no idea what I was doing." Keelin grabbed a second cup and poured herself some black tea. She blew on the cup as she settled at the table.

"Oh, I think you know more than you realize. You did a wonderful job of redirecting the illness."

"What was it? All I could see was this black twisty shape. It seemed to be invading his system."

"They think that he got into some of the poison they use to kill the rodents in the stables. It is quick acting and the chemist in town had nothing to reverse it. He had already vomited profusely but I believe that it had moved past that and was attacking his nervous system." Fiona shook her head at how close Finn had been to death.

"How do you know? How do you know what is the right thing to do? I was so scared," Keelin admitted.

"It is scary. Terrifying. You never know if you can do it or not. You have to tell people that too. All you can say is that you will try to help. There is never a guarantee. On anything, really." Fiona lifted her shoulders and let them fall. "I wish that I could give you a more definitive answer."

"What happened when I directed it out of the house? How could it have hit the tree? How could it, um, I don't know, become physical like that? What if I had hit someone outside?"

Fiona sighed. She moved to the table and sat down, looking into Keelin's face.

"I wish that I could truly tell you the science behind it, yet there is nothing that supports this. Trust me, I've looked. The old ways will tell you that as long as you direct it towards an inanimate object and your intentions are to dissolve it – not to harm another – it should be okay. I've had a few humdingers when I've directed it outside of windows, but I've yet to hit another person with it. You can tell it where to go, you know. If you have little to no place to direct it – send it up the chimney and out. Things like that. You can read through one of my books later on and learn a bit more about it."

"You realize that this is like, bat-shit crazy, right? I just can't get over this," Keelin blurted out.

"Keelin O'Brien. Do not use such language." Fiona eyed her. "And yes, it is crazy. Crazy beautiful though. This is the best gift. And the worst. You'll walk a fine line with this your whole life. Not all will be able to accept you. Be careful with whom you share your secrets. There is a difference between "dotty old woman who mixes up some healing tinctures" and "lay your hands upon someone and heal them." Know that. Understand that. This is nothing to mess with and you can easily be persecuted if the wrong group of people decide to judge you."

Fiona's words worried her. And she was absolutely right. Keelin tried to imagine performing a healing in Boston. They would carry her off and check her into the next loony bin.

"You'll want to increase your readings. I've pulled several books for you. No lessons for a few days. I think you had one of your biggest this morning. You'll need some time to absorb it all." Fiona motioned to a stack of books by the chairs in the small alcove.

"Okay, thanks. I want to head into town and talk to Cait; I think she is mad at me."

"Well, you shouldn't have kissed Shane," Fiona said dryly as she put away her teacup.

Shocked, Keelin whirled and looked at Fiona. A blush crept up her face and stained her cheeks.

"How did you know that? You weren't even home!"

"Word travels, my dear. As I told you, and you would do well to remember."

"Well, for one – he kissed me thankyouverymuch. And two, I told him that I just wanted to be friends and he tried anyway." Keelin felt righteously pissed off.

"Just friends, but you were wearing that little sundress on the date?"

"Hey, that was a perfectly acceptable dress for a dinner out." Though it may have shown a little more cleavage than attire for "just friends," Keelin thought. "Irrespective, it's nothing. We're nothing. And that's that."

"Mmhmm. You were doing it to get at Flynn. How'd that work out for you?"

Keelin sighed. She slumped back in her seat and began braiding her hair.

"He got mad at me. Then we fought. Now he is taking me out on his boat on Saturday. Which I haven't even agreed to go on yet."

"Ah, just like a man. Demanding. I bet he'll be a fine lover."

"Grandma! Oh my God."

"What? I've got eyes in my head don't I? That is one tall drink of water." Fiona laughed at her and the age dropped away from her face a little. Keelin could see that she had once been very beautiful.

"Was Grandpa a hottie?" Keelin asked.

"Oh my, child, he was delicious. Strong, broad shouldered, with hair that curled a bit in the rain. He was shy too, which I loved. I could always make him blush. Yet, in the bedroom, he was the one who made me blush."

Keelin choked on her tea. Fiona thumped her on the back as she struggled to breathe.

"He was the love of my life. For me there will be no other. Though I do so love having you here as well as that little pup. I had forgotten how nice it was to have an animal in the house." Fiona smiled fondly down at Ronan.

"It is nice. I've always wanted a dog. I've always wanted a brother or sister, in fact. Today was weird meeting Colin. He told me that he hated me!" Keelin said.

"I know, Keelin, I'm sorry. Though your dad loved Colin's mom, I don't think he ever truly got over losing you and Margaret. Kids are perceptive. He was a good dad but Colin and Aislinn always felt like they never quite lived up to the image they had of you. You'll have to break through that if you plan to have a relationship with them."

"How is that even fair? I was the one that got the short end. I had no brothers or sisters, no dad, and never even had a puppy." Keelin pouted. She had no idea how to deal with familial relations and she felt like she'd been unfairly judged.

"Who said it was fair? That's life. You're the one with more powers. Use them. You can heal in other ways, you know," Fiona said, and raised her eyebrows at Keelin.

It struck Keelin that she was right. She had taken "healing" to only be for physical ailments. She had never considered the potential for healing emotional rifts. Thinking back, she realized that she had always been the peacekeeper between her friends and the first phone call for those going through heartbreak. It was starting to make sense to her, this proclivity towards helping others.

"Did Colin bring the cars back? I need to go make things right with Cait."

"Yes, you do and yes, he did. Keys are in the front seat."

"Okay, I'll be back later. Do you need anything?"

Fiona waved her out.

"No, go on. Ronan and I are going to have a nice cup of tea and read a romance novel." Fiona laughed up at her and Keelin left for the village, shaking her head at this funny, lovely woman who had come into her life. Ireland was turning into a whole new adventure for her.

She parked close to Gallagher's pub and hoped that the early hour would offer up a relatively empty pub. She needed to set a few things straight with Cait.

Keelin entered the cheerful building and squinted into the warm light, letting her eyes adjust as she scanned the room. A few tables held some older men playing cards and talking sports. Cait stood behind the worn bar, drying glasses. Not much taller than the bar, her slender build seemed dwarfed by it. Catching sight of Keelin, she narrowed her eyes at her and turned to go into the kitchen.

"Cait, wait. Please."

Cait stopped, huffed out a breath, and turned back to the bar. She put on a polite smile.

"Can I get you something to drink?"

"Sure, I'll have a Bulmers." Keelin eased herself onto a stool at the empty bar and watched the slim brunette carefully pour her a cider. She wanted to make sure Cait didn't spit in it.

"Listen, Cait, I didn't know. Honestly. I just got to town. I thought I may have seen interest the other night but neither of you said a word to me. And I'm not interested in Shane. He's a nice guy but he isn't for me." Keelin rushed the words out.

Cait huffed out a breath. Never one to hold a temper for long, she smiled at Keelin.

"Okay, thanks. I don't even know why I lose my head over that man. Not that he even pays me that much attention. And when he does it certainly isn't by taking me out to nice seafood dinners or kissing me in the car." Cait looked at Keelin sideways as she stocked glasses.

"Does everyone know about the kiss?" Keelin threw up her hands in exasperation.

"Liam told Sarah who told me." Cait laughed at her.

"I don't even know these people. This is just ridiculous." She took a big gulp of her drink and let the cider cool her throat.

"Oh, get used to it if you live here. Everyone is in everyone else's business. Why don't you like Shane?" Cait blurted out.

"Oh, I do. I really do. I think he gets a bad reputation or tries to portray himself as something that he isn't. But I think he's lonely, to be honest. Either way, there's no chemistry. At least not with him." Keelin stopped herself. She mentally kicked herself and reminded herself of the town's need to gossip.

"Ah, does a certain dark-haired neighbor with the best shoulders in the county have you a little more interested?" Cait said intuitively.

"No, of course not." Keelin looked down at her drink.

"Bullshit."

"Damn it. Okay, but you can't say anything. Swear to it, Cait. If we are to be friends – real girlfriends – you can't say a word. Promise." Keelin needed someone to talk to. Her grandma was a sweetheart but she didn't think she could get down to the nitty gritty with her.

"Only if you promise never to kiss Shane again."

"Done."

"Okay, so tell me, is he as good in bed as he looks?" Cait leaned eagerly over the bar, crossing her arms on the bar rail.

"What! No, we haven't. I mean, not that." Keelin blushed. "We've messed around a little, but we haven't had sex."

"And why not? Are you blind? I want to lap that man up like a bucket of cream." Cait made yummy-sounding noises.

"Oh, he's gorgeous. And infuriating. He always sees me at my worst and I feel like such a klutz around him." Keelin filled Cait in on all the times that Flynn had come to her rescue. Cait's eyes went dreamy and she heaved a big sigh. She fluttered her hand at her breasts.

"Ah, a big strong man coming to my rescue all the time? Sign me up! Maybe that is my problem with Shane. I need to be more helpless around him." Cait sighed.

"It wasn't intentional. And it just pissed me off. You know, back in Boston, I am a relatively capable individual. This has just been a series of incidents since I've gotten here and that man has witnessed every last one," Keelin fumed into her cider.

"Doesn't sound like a bad problem to have. He's a good guy, you know. He does a lot for the community and he looks after your granny just right."

"He's taking me on his boat Saturday. If I go."

Cait slammed a glass on the bar and stared at her.

"His boat? Like his real boat? Not the fishing boat? He doesn't take anyone on that boat."

"What boat? I have no idea. He said his boat. I didn't get details as I was busy yelling at him at the time."

"Okay, you have to tell me this now." Cait leaned eagerly on the bar and propped her face in her hands.

Keelin told her about their argument and how furious she had been at Flynn for making demands on her yet not treating her like a lady or courting her. Cait whistled.

"Keelin, he doesn't take anyone on his boat. Calling it a boat is like calling a Porsche a sedan. It is the one real luxury he allows himself. He docks around the side of the cove and we rarely see it. You have to give me full details. Oh, I'm dying to hear what it looks like inside. You have to seduce him below deck so I can get details."

Keelin eyed her balefully.

"Oh, sure, I'll be sure to throw myself at him so you can hear what kind of finishings his boat has."

"Yes! Do it. I'd do it for you but he treats me like a sister."

"Um, excuse me, what about this Shane guy?"

"Oh, I know, I know. Flynn isn't for me. But I can dream, can't I? Yummy. What are you going to wear? Are you getting your hair done? Maybe not. You don't want to look like you tried too hard."

Keelin stared at her as Cait chattered on. Nerves started ticking in her stomach. Was this a real date? What was she going to wear? Would he expect her to put out? It was all she could think of anyway. She groaned. She was toast.

"I'm screwed."

"Girl, you are so screwed. Both literally and figuratively. I can't wait for details."

Keelin flicked an ice cube at her and laughed. It was nice to have a girlfriend to gossip with even if the subject matter terrified her. As she drove home that night, she wondered what she would do. Would she sleep with Flynn? She wasn't a virgin, yet her last relationship had been over two years ago. Never one for casual sex, she'd mainly abstained since then. Which was probably why she was ready to explode, she thought. Lack of regular sex could cloud a person's brain. It must just be that. Send the resident fantasy guy in to get her juices flowing. That was all it was and nothing more. And maybe a fling would be good for her, she mused. It seemed like this summer was going to be full of a bunch of firsts for her; she might as well have some fun with it.

Chapter Sixteen

KEELIN WOKE AFTER another night of fitful dreams. This time it wasn't Flynn that filled her dreams so much as the visions of trees exploding and a sick child crying. She was going to have to come to terms with this gift of hers, she thought.

Though her date with Flynn wasn't until Saturday, she could hear Cait's voice in her head and buried her head in her closet.

"I have nothing to wear on a boat date. Not a single thing," Keelin declared to Ronan, who watched her eagerly. She knew it wasn't true but, hey, if there ever was a time for vanity – it was now.

She decided that today would be a perfect day to check out the shops in town and she hoped to drop in on her sister. The thought made her nervous but she kept thinking of Fiona's words about her power to heal and how it wasn't just for sickness. She needed to build her confidence if she was to be a healer, she decided. And, what better way to do that than to stride right into uncomfortable family situations?

Leaving Ronan to play with Fiona in the garden, Keelin drove into town, taking the winding cliff road with the sea views. She turned the radio up and sang her heart out to some bad 80s music. There were only a few near misses with cars when she forgot to drive in the left lane and overall she congratulated herself on a successful trip into the village. *I can get the hang of this,* she thought.

Keelin made her way to the little downtown, packed with small shops. After maneuvering a parking spot and taking far longer to parallel park on the left side than she prided herself on doing in Boston, she got out and stretched. The fun part first or the unknown? Deciding to tackle the hardest part first, she made her way to Aislinn's shop. It was mid-morning and bound to be open. Keelin approached the shop and eyed it critically. It was small and painted a butter yellow on the outside. Deep brown wood beams crisscrossed the window frames and outlined the thick door. Cheerful window boxes full of red flowers invited people inside and a window display of intricate lace and watery paintings spoke to a passerby's soul. The entire picture was inviting and Keelin smiled. Her sister must have a good head for business. She hung around outside for a bit but, remembering the village's knack for gossip, realized she was probably creating a scene. Briskly, she opened the door and small bells tinkled at her entrance.

"I was wondering how long you planned to stand out there. I've received two phone calls as is." A voice like honey reached out to her from somewhere across the beautiful room. Keelin didn't know where to look first, from the collection of black-and-white photography framed in driftwood that cluttered the walls, to the intricately spun lace that hung from racks throughout the room. Talent was evident in the work displayed here. Keelin wound through the racks towards the voice.

Aislinn stood at a workbench with her back to Keelin and hammered a small wooden frame. Satisfied, she put her hammer down, wiped her hands on her work apron, and turned to greet Keelin.

"Hello, sis." Aislinn's mouth quirked. She was a study in contrasts. A strong build, yet not overweight, her trim pants and button-down shirt showed soft curves. Her eyes mirrored the shape of Keelin's, yet the light of the ocean reflected there instead. Her round cheeks contrasted with a wide mouth and a sharp chin. Deep brown hair tumbled in waves over her shoulders and at least two pencils were twined in the mass.

Aislinn held out her hand to greet Keelin. There wasn't warmth here. Yet, there wasn't animosity, either. Aislinn silently measured Keelin.

"Yes, sisters, so it seems. The first I've heard of it." Keelin held out her hand and grasped a strong, yet smooth, hand and shook it lightly.

"Ah, so Colin's said. Surprise!" Aislinn raised her eyebrows and gestured towards the teapot. "Tea?"

"Yes, thank you."

Aislinn busied herself with pouring tea into two thick blue cups, lightly glazed with a pattern of white. They were lovely and Keelin suspected they were homemade. She said as much.

"Ah, yes, for a brief moment in time I fancied myself a potter. I've moved on since then." Aislinn gestured with her cup at the various types of art that cluttered the studio. If she was a study in contrasts as a person, her art mirrored that taste exactly. From soft watercolors to edgy black-and-white photos, Keelin was surprised the same person had created it.

"All of this is yours?"

"Yes, I have trouble staying focused on one thing for long."

Keelin walked the room and examined the various displays. She knew immediately the lace doilies she would be sending home to Margaret and set those aside. She stopped in front of a black-and-white picture of Grace's Cove. Taken late in the afternoon, Aislinn had captured the rising moon and the setting sun in one photo. It was stunning and Keelin had to have it.

"This is amazing. I must have it. How much?"

Aislinn studied her for a moment. "You know, for a long time I hated you. It was only recently that I began to pity you."

"Pity me? Why?" Keelin ran her hands through her hair. She was no good at these family relationship things.

162

She took a deep breath and tried to call on her other power to muddle through this.

"Of course. The great Keelin. The apple of my father's eyes. His little girl. You weren't there to fight with so you were easy to hate. I've decided to be mature though and look at things from another perspective. You had no father at all. I suppose that wasn't easy either," Aislinn said casually as she tucked a picture in a frame and finished sealing the back of it. "Plus, you healed Finnegan. So, I'm prepared to like you for that alone."

Keelin recognized her second olive branch of the week. She breathed a sigh of relief.

"Well, I can tell you that I've always wanted a family. I wanted a sister or brother. Someone else for my mother to focus her attention on. Without a husband, or other kids, I was my mom's only focus. It's not easy to live in that situation. I never even got to have a puppy. Now I come to Ireland and I have two siblings and a dog in a matter of weeks. I'm trying to roll with the punches, but this has all been a little overwhelming for me. I guess I came here hoping to, I don't know, just get to know you a little bit. I don't expect us to be sisters or anything." Keelin rushed it out before she got too nervous to say it all.

Aislinn studied her.

"I guess that makes sense. I don't really know what to do with you either."

They both burst out laughing. Aislinn walked over to the picture of Grace's Cove and took it off the wall and handed it to Keelin.

"Here. A welcome gift of sorts. Welcome."

Keelin was touched. It was a stunning photograph, and a quick peek at the price revealed it not to be cheap either.

"Thank you, I'll treasure it always. So, does this mean we can be friends?"

Aislinn nodded. "I'd like that. I think. As long as you aren't too bitchy or high maintenance. Colin's super stressed out all the time and I can't always deal. I need my alone time and I need to let my creative flow...well, flow."

"I could see that. Colin did seem wound a little tight. Though he'd just gone through a pretty stressful experience."

Aislinn turned and looked into Keelin's eyes.

"So, what's the deal with all that? How can you do that?" Keelin was startled yet she saw more than curiosity in Aislinn's eyes. Aislinn really wanted to know.

"I'm still figuring that out, I guess. I don't even know what it's all about. This is Fiona's thing but it seems like I have a knack for it. Or something. I don't really know." Noncommittal, she watched Aislinn as she nervously played with a silver chain around her neck. Since they were sisters, she decided to be blunt.

"Do you have this too? Can you heal?"

Aislinn dropped her necklace and straightened quickly.

"No, no. Why would you say that? Of course not." She didn't meet Keelin's eyes. Keelin pounced.

"You do! You have something." Without thinking she grabbed Aislinn's hand and read her. Images flooded her head of a young girl who saw colors around people and drew them.

"Are you empathic?" Keelin asked.

Aislinn sighed. "I should have known that I wouldn't be able to keep my secret from you. I could tell right away when you came in. Your power is strong, as is your light."

"Tell me. Tell me everything. I'm dying to know." They were interrupted by the bell at the door and Aislinn hurried to meet her customer. Keelin wandered the shop and thought about what she had learned. Would this mean that her brother had some sort of power, wait, no Fiona had said it was females only. So, who else in the village had these powers? How many were descendants of Grace? Keelin had a million questions. As more customers came in, she knew the time for questions would be later.

Catching Aislinn's eye, she motioned to the picture and pile of lace. "I'll be back for this. I'm going to go shopping." Aislinn waved her out and Keelin walked up the road towards Gallagher's Pub. It was still early enough that maybe Cait could take a break and go shopping with her. She needed some normalcy in her life.

Keelin found Cait reading the newspaper at the empty bar.

"Psst, can you take an hour? I need an outfit."

Cait jumped up and threw her fist in the air.

"Yes! Girl's day! I need this. I want to make Shane drool. Let's get our nails done too." Quickly throwing the closed sign in the pub window, Cait looked out the door and rubbed her hands together in anticipation. "Where first?"

Keelin laughed at her. "That didn't take much convincing. You lead the way. It appears that I need something to wear on a boat."

"Oh, we are going to sex you up. Let's go." She dragged Keelin down the road towards a small boutique that had dresses on the mannequins in the front window.

"I'm thinking short and tight. That way whenever you step over something on the boat or bend over, he'll drool. You can wear super sexy underwear." Petite Cait obviously didn't have some of the body issues that Keelin had.

"Um, Cait. No. I'm not as small as you. I can't do short or tight. It's just, well, it shows my tummy and I've got large hips."

Cait turned to Keelin with her mouth open.

"Shut up! You have the perfect hourglass figure. I would die for your curves. I am straight up and down like a little boy. I've always hated girls like you. You can fill out a dress. They hang on me."

"What! I've always hated girls like you. You never have to think about muffin top or if the store carries your size."

They stared at each other and started laughing.

"Okay, let's meet in the middle. I'll go fitted, but maybe longer. I don't need to be showing off my hoo-ha all night."

Cait shrieked in laughter and started pulling dresses.

"Oh, this one is lovely. Try this. It's just the right amount of casual and sexy. Try it, try it." Cait handed her a brilliant red dress that flowed to the floor.

"Red? I never wear red. It won't go with my hair."

"What? Have you tried it? It would be perfect with your eyes and your skin tone. Plus, your hair is more of a blonde than red. Just try it."

Keelin went into the dressing room and eyed the dress. It was certainly out of her comfort zone. Thank God it wasn't strapless, she thought. Sighing, she pulled the dress on over her head, and tugged it down, feeling it bunch on her chest and then hug her waist down over her butt. She turned and looked in the mirror and gasped.

"Let me see!" Cait ripped the curtain open.

"It's…it's..."

"It's stunning. Oh, he is going to fall over when he sees you."

The dress was a curious mixture of loose and tight. It reminded Keelin of the dresses that girls on *Real Housewives of Miami* wore. It was beachy, sexy, nighttime and casual all in one. Wide straps covered her broad shoulders and tapered into a deep V in the front, dipping even lower in the back. It hid everything that needed to be hidden and showed everything it should. It was, quite simply, the perfect dress on her. Keelin laughed and watched herself in the mirror. The red brought out a flush in her cheeks and made her hair color pop. She looked alive and sexy.

"Oh, Flynn is going to eat you alive."

Keelin gulped. "Um, maybe this dress is a bit much. I don't want to give the wrong impression."

"This dress gives all the right impressions, trust me. He's not going to be able to speak all night."

"That's what I'm afraid of."

Suddenly protective, Cait grabbed her arm. "Is this too much? Are you ready for this date? We can find you something else a little more subdued if you want."

Keelin turned and looked at the woman in the mirror. This woman was confident. Sure of herself. Sexy, sensual, and in control. She wanted to be this woman. She could be this woman. She gave herself a small nod.

"Let's consider this a confidence-building exercise. Flynn is toast."

Cait barked out a laugh. "Go get him, girl. I can't wait to hear about this."

Later that day, Keelin made her way back to Aislinn's shop. She found her closing up for the day.

"Want to grab a pint?" Aislinn asked her as she finished packaging Keelin's lace and picture.

"Sure. Up at Cait's pub or elsewhere?"

"How about right here?" Aislinn laughed at her as she flipped the sign closed and gestured to a refrigerator in back. "Less gossip this way."

Relieved, Keelin headed for the fridge and pulled out two bottles of Harp. Aislinn motioned towards the back door and she opened it to reveal a small, enclosed courtyard. A worn yellow brick wall surrounded the small yard that was brimming with flowers. Intricate statues and various lawn ornaments were woven through the flowers. A large planked table stood in the middle covered in sketchbooks and jars of art supplies. Aislinn brushed them aside and put down a plate of cookies that she had brought out with her.

"I know there is a bunch of time to catch up on who we are and what we do and all that, but I'm dying to know about your power. I'm really struggling to learn about mine," Keelin said in a rush of breath. She grabbed a cookie and quickly crammed it in her mouth, hoping to stem the flow of words.

Aislinn laughed and gazed across the courtyard. She fiddled with a pencil on the table and sighed. "I guess that I don't really know when or how I've really defined them. I haven't met anyone like me therefore I rarely talk about it. I don't take it for granted but I don't always know how to describe what I do and don't know about myself."

Keelin nodded and gestured with her Harp bottle. "Go on."

"I don't really think I know when it started. I don't think I realized that I was different from other people until my parents started training me not to talk about certain things. I could always see colors around people. I would run up to them and tell them that I liked their purple color and people would look at me like I was crazy." Aislinn laughed and took a swing of her beer.

"So, you see auras? What else? What is all incorporated with that?"

169

"Well, I finally realized that one of the reasons I am so sensitive is that I can feel what other people are feeling. I can read them at a hundred paces. I'll know if someone is lying, happy, sad, or angry. That's why I decided to withhold judgment on you until I actually met you. Well, I shouldn't say "withhold" but at least I was willing to give you a chance." Aislinn laughed at Keelin.

"That's okay. I understand. Hey, I only learned about you both this week so I haven't had much time for any judgments. I'm taking it as is. Though I may have a few words with my dear mother for omitting this information."

"I really can't believe she never told you. It's fascinating to me," Aislinn said as she idly drew a sketch of Keelin on her pad.

"My mother has a tendency of avoiding unpleasant discussions. I imagine this was one of those that she liked to sweep under the rug. A pretty big sweep, mind you. It wasn't until Fiona sent for me that she even acknowledged Grace's Cove and that there might be some sort of power there."

Aislinn nodded. "I get it. She wants the best for her girl. Society isn't kind to those who are touched with a little extra something. That must have been tough growing up."

"It was." Keelin swallowed over the lump in her throat. It was so nice to finally talk openly about this. "I cried when my mom finally acknowledged that she knew that I had a gift. I felt like it was something that was to be shunned and hidden. I don't think that I have ever felt as alive as I have since I've come to Ireland."

"I'm sorry. I always had Fiona. She was kind to me and taught me how to nurture myself without showing the whole world my gift. She saved me," Aislinn said ruefully as she continued to sketch on her pad.

"I think that I understand. She is saving me right now. I feel like I've never felt as much true emotion as I have in the past few weeks. It is just pouring from me. It is over-whelming. But. Discovering my power? Finally not hiding from it? God, it is exhilarating. I feel energized," Keelin admitted.

"Yes, there is something about stepping into your own that just kind of makes your soul sing, right? That is how I feel with my shop. The happiest day of my life was bor-rowing money to start this place. I've never regretted it. A traditional job would never have fit me. I can't handle of-fice work or being around that many people all day every day. This works perfectly for me," Aislinn said as she took a swig from her bottle of Harp.

"So how does this whole empathic thing affect dating?" Keelin asked, and snagged another cookie from the plate.

"Ugh." Aislinn groaned and took another swig of her beer. "It's not pretty. It takes some of that mental guess-work – that spice out of it. I can read people fairly clearly so if a man is guilty or trying to hide anything – I know it immediately. I also know if he is interested in another woman or doesn't really love me. It makes it tricky. I also don't reveal that side of myself to many. I just pour that all into my work."

Keelin nodded. "Which is beautiful by the way. You should sell this overseas."

Aislinn shrugged. "I may. I don't know yet. I sell across Ireland and make a sustainable living for now. We'll see where that takes me. Now. Tell me how you healed Finn."

Keelin opened her mouth and stopped. She thought about how to explain what she didn't herself understand. "I don't really know. I am only just exploring this ability. I've had weird things happen to me growing up but Mom never acknowledged it and I just kind of wrote it off. But I also felt like there was a part of me missing. Since being here, I feel like my soul is humming, if that makes sense?"

"It does. You aren't hiding from yourself anymore."

Keelin raised her beer bottle. "Exactly!"

"Yeah, I get you. It's nice to be able to talk about this with someone." Aislinn offered Keelin her first unguarded smile. "I think we'll get along just fine, sis." They clinked bottles and made plans to meet up later that week.

"So, Flynn? Are you going to sleep with him?" Aislinn met her eyes.

Keelin looked at her quietly. "I don't know. I want to."

"I can see that you are a mess of feelings. Love usually is complicated, you know."

"I don't love him!" Keelin gaped at her.

Aislinn gave her an enigmatic smile and rose to clear their bottles. She said nothing and walked inside.

"I don't!" Keelin called after her. Silence answered her.

Chapter Seventeen

KEELIN TOOK THE cliff drive home. The fading sun cast a warm glow over the cliffs and the romance of Ireland seeped into her bones. There was nothing casual about Ireland's beauty. It was weepy, mystical, and oftentimes a punch to the heart. Keelin idly daydreamed about living here, nestled amongst the hills, with a child of her own to nurture. Shocked, she snapped out of her daydream. A child? She had never considered herself a maternal type. Where had that thought come from? Keelin shook her head as she pulled into the cottage's drive.

The warm scents of an Irish stew greeted her as she pushed the door open. Fiona tended a pot at the stove and smiled at her as she added more spices to the bubbling liquid. Ronan yipped and raced across the floor to greet her, tumbling over himself and sprawling haphazardly on her feet. Keelin laughed down at him and scratched his belly, murmuring nonsense words to him.

"A graceful one he is not." Fiona laughed at him from the stove. "Are you hungry?"

"Yes, please, I'd love to eat." Keelin helped to set the table with some warm brown bread and heavy stoneware bowls. Fiona bustled over and poured the steaming soup into the bowls. She inhaled and gave a brisk nod.

"Perfect. Now, tell me about your day."

Between bites of the chunky stew, Keelin filled Fiona in on most of her day. When she got to Aislinn's powers, she stopped. She wasn't sure if Aislinn would like her discussing her powers with Fiona. She didn't want to violate any sort of sister code.

Fiona eyed her. "Ah, I see Aislinn must have told you about her."

Keelin blew out a breath. "Yes. She did. Is it okay to talk about it?"

"Yes, with me it is. I've been one of the few that she could talk to freely. I did my best to lead her on a path of exploring her talents while still trying to lead a normal life. Lucky for her, the creative talents she has offered a wonderful outlet for much of her powers."

"Okay, so I just have to ask. Who all is a descendent of Grace? Does everyone have powers that are? Is it just us? What about Colin?"

Fiona eyed her levelly. "No. It is only passed down through the women. Colin is not gifted. Your friend Cait is."

"What! Cait is? What does she have?"

Fiona tapped her head.

"What? What does that mean? Minds? She can read minds?" Keelin's mouth dropped open as she stared at Fiona.

Fiona nodded and cleared the stoneware from the table to the sink. As she rinsed the dishes she motioned towards the cabinet. "Let's have a whiskey."

Silently agreeing that they needed a little something, Keelin pulled out a bottle of Clontarf and poured them both a generous portion. Together, they settled in the nook by the small fire and Ronan leaped onto her lap. Keelin picked up her glass and examined its contents. The fire picked up the warm gold of the whiskey and it seemed to glow from within. Keelin couldn't meet Fiona's eyes.

"I feel like I am going a little crazy. I am really struggling with understanding how I am able to do what I do. I had a nightmare last night about that tree exploding. On the other hand, part of my soul feels like it is singing because I am finally in the right spot for me."

Fiona smiled and took a sip of her whiskey. She rocked softly in her chair and leaned over to stir the fire. "Keelin, dear. This is very overwhelming. It is normal for you to feel this way. I wish that I had gotten to you sooner so I could have helped you to understand yourself as you grew. I wish that I had a distinct answer for you on what this power is but all I can tell you is my own conclusions that I have reached. I truly believe this power comes from a universal energy that we can all tap into. However, some of us are given the ability to tap into it where others have to actively work at it. Maybe it is from God, or maybe it is just a source energy. I only know that which I am compelled to do and that is to help others. From that alone I can only believe it is a power that is meant to be."

"But, what about being a descendant of Grace? The cove? How is that all tied in?"

"Ah, yes. Well, when Grace was close to her death she went into seclusion. Her oldest daughter went with her. Together, they decided on the final resting place for Grace. For months prior to her death, Grace and her daughter would spend the night at the cove and chant under the light of the moon. Now, this is powerful sorcery that I am talking about here – magic. Her daughter was pregnant at the time and absorbed much of this magic. When Grace was close to dying, she shared her blood with her daughter in a sacred ritual of blessing and passing of her power. Shortly after she gave her power away, she passed on and was burned on a funeral pyre at the cove. The story goes that her daughter swam to the pyre and collected the ashes in the chalice before hiding it deep in a small cave far out in the cove. There are so many charms and protections on the cove that nobody has been able to reach the cave. They all die while trying. It is said that her daughter gave birth the evening Grace died. It is believed that her soul lives on through her granddaughter and descendants."

Keelin let out a deep breath she had been holding. Her science mind warred with what she had seen of the power of the cove. "What do you mean give away her power? Can you do that?"

"Of course, Keelin." Fiona looked at her. "Look at your mother. She never formally renounced her power yet she chooses to live as if it doesn't exist. In doing so, she'll never find true happiness. It is a difficult trade-off. She lives in fear of what she truly is and turns her back on her power. Would she just claim it and learn to harness it, happiness would be hers."

"Is this why I've always felt so unsettled? I've never claimed my power?" Keelin took a small sip of her whiskey and rubbed Ronan's back. The pup stretched lazily in her lap and rolled onto his back, revealing his stomach to Keelin. She smiled at him and felt her heart ache a bit with love for the small dog.

"Yes. But, in some respects, don't you think that goes for anyone? Think about the people who are accountants or businessmen that simply follow what their parents or wives want for them. They don't follow what makes them feel good, what their true passion is, and with that, a part of them dies. If they would just step into their power they would know true happiness."

"Are you happy?" Keelin asked Fiona.

Fiona took a small sip of her whiskey and stared at the flames. "Yes, I am. Though I don't think I could ever say that I know one way or the other. It isn't a thought process. It isn't an up and down. I don't know how to be happy because I am happy. Everyone in the States is constantly striving to be happy, obsessing about it really, and

177

nobody realizes that they are standing in their own way. Happiness can be an existence, not just a mood. I've always likened it to simply pivoting when things make me feel negative. If something feels bad to me, I pivot away from it and move towards what makes me feel good. I do this irrespective of what others think. Most don't know how to live that way."

Keelin nodded. She thought about how she had felt when she had healed Finn. It was a mixture of sheer terror along with a rush of power. Part of her had liked it. Almost too much. She decided to voice her concerns to Fiona. "I, well, when I healed Finn, it just, it was kind of awesome. It scared me but at the same time it made me giddy! I wanted to run around and make flowers bloom and heal people who were coughing on the street. I don't know if I like that side of myself though. It seems, almost, I don't know, cocky?"

Fiona smiled at her and leaned over to pat Ronan's head. "You're a good girl, Keelin. That was actually one of my biggest concerns when Margaret cut off contact. I feared that you would discover your power and get greedy in your use of it. But, as you know, power carries responsibility. And, the healer's gift can also be their greatest curse. Used inappropriately, your power will kill you." Fiona met and held her eyes. Keelin inhaled a shaky breath and nodded.

"So, some of this needed to happen the way it did."

"Ah yes, to everything in its own time." Fiona raised her glass and clinked it with Keelin's. They both sipped their whiskey and stared at the flames as the shadows grew deep at the window.

"Do you think we should try to find the chalice?" Keelin blurted out. The cove haunted her dreams and she didn't know why.

"Good lord, girl. No. You've heard the term 'let sleeping dogs lie' right? Let this dog sleep."

"I know. I know. I do. It, it is just so fascinating." Keelin quickly backpedaled.

"How many times does the cove need to try to kill you before your realize that not everything in life is meant to be answered? There are some things that are greater than answers. I know your science mind struggles with that but you must leave the chalice in peace. It is where it needs to be. To disrupt that would be catastrophic." Fiona stared at her with an unwavering gaze.

"But, why does the cove glow blue all the time? It drives me crazy!" Keelin blurted out.

Fiona gasped. "You're in love with Flynn!" A smile broke out on the older woman's face and she jumped from her seat to do a quick jig.

"What? No. No, I am not. Whatever made you say that?" Keelin felt warmth spreading through her cheeks.

"Ah, my dear heart, you most certainly are. I thought that you had only seen it the one time with me. But if you've seen it around Flynn that is very different. A very little known fact about Grace O'Malley is that she was a romantic at heart. A brutal woman to the bone, she believed in love to her dying day. While the cove often glows

179

for its own or when someone passes it will always glow in the presence of love. It did for me with your grandfather." Fiona danced around the room with Ronan barking at her heels. "We will plan the loveliest wedding on the hills."

"Whoa, whoa, whoa. Stop. No wedding. No anything. I don't even know how I feel about Flynn. I've only been here a few weeks. And I certainly do not plan on marrying anytime soon."

Fiona smiled at her. "Ah, the stubbornness of youth. There is no time frame on love."

"Um, does he know about, well, about the powers we have?"

Fiona returned to her seat and took a happy gulp of her whiskey.

"Why don't you ask him?"

"I can't ask him! What – just say hey by the way I can heal people with my hands? Are you cool with that?" Keelin threw up her hands and shook her head at Ronan. He panted up at her with his pink tongue hanging from his mouth.

"Love does not include lies. Either the man accepts you as a whole or he is not the man for you."

"But, I don't even know my whole self." Keelin felt dangerously close to tears. The person she had known in Boston was gone. She wasn't sure of this new Keelin yet but she wanted to keep learning. But to open her heart to love without fully knowing herself – she was certain that would bring nothing but a destructive end.

"You'll get there. And, you'd be surprised what a man in love can help you to discover about yourself. Now, I'm for bed. You stay up and enjoy the rest of the fire. Take some time to think about what you want." Fiona leaned over and pressed her weathered lips to Keelin's smooth cheek. "You've a good heart, Keelin. Let it guide you."

Keelin was dangerously afraid that she knew exactly where her big heart would lead her and it wasn't onto a plane back to Boston. She groaned and leaned her head back against the chair as she stared at the fire. What was she doing with her life? In a matter of weeks she had a whole new family, a pet, and potentially a love life. Her newfound healing talent left her in awe and her studies for school no longer seemed to interest her. She wanted to learn how to be a true healer, not a marine biologist. And, if she admitted it, she'd never felt happier. Flynn's face popped into her head. Her stomach tingled as she thought about her date with him. She wanted him. There was no denying that – but love? There was so much to learn about him. And what about the important things like if he ate pizza or snored at night? All those little details that made people compatible. Shouldn't she know some of these things before her heart said she was in love? Deciding that denial was a safe bet, Keelin tamped the fire down and finished her whiskey, hoping the warmth would lull her into sleep.

Chapter Eighteen

THE NEXT DAY Keelin went into town early. She wanted to catch Cait before she opened the pub. Determined to find out more about her new friend, Keelin devised a plan on the drive in. Unfortunately, her mind kept scattering to her big date later that evening.

It's not a big date, Keelin reminded herself. She hadn't seen Flynn since he had stormed off through the fields all Lord of the Manor and whatnot. She assumed that was part of his strategy because now all she did was think about him. Well, about him and her newfound power. Both consumed her and left shadows under her eyes from restless nights. Part of her felt raw, like she was being born into a new skin. It seemed to her like there was no gradual testing of the waters with anything since she had arrived in Ireland. Power flooded her just as much as lust did. Keelin felt like she was lit from within.

Luck was on her side and a parking spot was open directly in front of the pub. Keelin checked the clock. At 11:00, the pub would be open but not quite serving lunch yet. Perfect, she thought. She hoped that her plan worked.

Keelin opened the door quietly and walked inside. She squinted her eyes into the dim light of the pub and saw Cait with her back to the door stacking glasses on the bar. Keelin stood where she was. "What is your soup of the day?" she asked in her head – not out loud.

"A lovely vegetable barley is on the pot for you," Cait said as she turned and smiled. She stopped and dropped a glass to the counter as she looked into Keelin's eyes. Her mouth dropped open.

"I didn't say that out loud, Cait." Keelin moved towards the bar.

"Oh, feck. I should've known you would figure it out." Cait sighed and hunched her shoulders. "Go on, run on. I know you will think I'm a freak."

"What? No!" Keelin was shocked. She hurried around the bar and ducked under the pass-through. She pulled the small woman into her arms. "No, please don't think that. I don't feel that way at all. I'm sorry. I should have just asked you. I shouldn't have pulled that trick on you."

She felt Cait tense in her arms. She shuddered out a deep breath before she gave a small nod. Stepping back, Cait smiled up at Keelin.

"It's okay. I'm just so used to hiding it. Come on, you should really try the soup." Cait ushered her towards a seat.

Keelin let out a breath and pulled up a stool at the bar. She was relieved that she hadn't hurt her friend too badly. She should have thought her plan through. What had she been thinking?

"I said it's okay." Cait laughed at her as Keelin jumped a bit.

"Okay, this will be something that I have to get used to. But, well, you know about me, right?" Keelin asked as she glanced over her shoulder for other patrons.

"Yes, I know. I wondered when you would feel comfortable sharing with me," Cait said as she slid a cup of tea in front of Keelin.

"I guess, I don't know, I guess I am still just trying to figure it all out. How does having this power work for you? I can't read minds but if I grab someone's hand I can get flashes of them or their past. Obviously, if they are sick I can read that." Keelin blew on her tea and idly stirred some milk into her cup.

"I don't know, not really. I had a hard time growing up because it took me a long time to figure out that people weren't always speaking what I would hear from them. Thank God for Fiona. She taught me how to shield myself. Frankly, if it wasn't for her I would never be able to work in a crowded bar. Now, I rarely hear people's thoughts unless I actively tune in or if I am alone and unguarded." Cait wiped the counter down and continued to do the busywork of setting up the bar stations. Keelin sipped her tea and gestured with the cup for her to continue. "Honestly, I think that most people have forgotten that I can read minds or choose to ignore it. But it makes dating difficult."

"I was going to ask about that. So, does Shane really like you?"

Cait threw up her hands. "Ugh, I don't know! I try to be respectful of him and not poke into his brain. Interestingly enough, he is one of the hardest people to read that I've come across. I think that is part of his appeal."

"He's a kind man, you know. I read him."

Cait nodded. "I know, I can tell. Plus I had Aislinn read his colors. He's a pure one. Unfortunately, my thoughts about him are anything but." Cait grinned at her wickedly and Keelin barked out a laugh.

"Girl, go after him."

"Uh huh. Just like you are going after Flynn?" Cait raised her eyebrow at her.

Keelin gulped her tea. "God, I'm so nervous. What am I doing with that man?"

"I hope it involves handcuffs." Cait shrieked with laughter as Keelin's mouth dropped open. "You should see your face."

"I, jeez." Keelin huffed out a breath and fanned her face. The mental images of Flynn with handcuffs were enough to make her squirm. "Have you ever dated him?"

"Flynn? Gosh no. Not for lack of trying though." Cait smiled at her. "Honestly though, Flynn doesn't date in the village, to the dismay of many a broken heart. He likes to keep his home life and love life separate. So, lucky for you, you'll not have any jealous exes coming after you here."

"Well that's something, I guess. I'm nervous," Keelin confessed in a rush of words. "It's been a long time for me and I just about lose my head when that man is around me. I don't know how it will be."

"Listen to your heart. You'll know if it isn't right for you," Cait said.

"That's what I'm afraid of. Listening to my heart. I feel like I don't know myself and at the same time like I finally know myself." Keelin twirled her spoon in her teacup.

"Well, I know one man who wants to get to know you. Why don't you really talk to him tonight and take some time to get to know him? You might have a better sense of things after that. If he doesn't already have you undressed below deck by then." Fiona shot her a smile as Keelin groaned.

"You know, part of that thought freaks me out and the other part really wants it."

"Listen to the part that wants it." Cait raised her glass to Keelin.

Chapter Nineteen

KEELIN MULLED OVER Cait's advice on the way home to get ready for her date. She was right. Keelin needed to get out of her head and into her heart. Keelin caught herself humming along to the radio as she navigated the cliff roads. It was a strange feeling – this coming into her own. Boston seemed like worlds away. Being out from under her mother's scrutiny and away from the need to finish school had freed her in a way that she may have never known. Under Fiona's tutelage she was slowly learning an entirely new craft that made her soul sing. For that alone she was grateful. For the hunky neighbor next door that she wanted to devour in one gulp? She wasn't sure if grateful was the word exactly. She decided to embrace the evening and listen to her heart and only her heart. Let it lead her where she needed to be.

Keelin laughed as she pulled into the drive. Flynn's dog stood to attention with a basket of flowers in her mouth. That man did not miss a trick, she thought as she bounded out of the car to take the basket in her hands. A small card was tucked amongst the wildflower blossoms. Keelin leaned over and rubbed the scruff on Teagan's neck. "Go on, girl. You can tell him that I got the basket." She smiled as Teagan took off over the hills. Just add that to the list of weird things here, she thought. Keelin tucked the basket under her arm and ripped the card open as she nudged the door with her hip.

"Though lovely and fair as the rose of the summer
Yet, 'twas not her beauty alone that won me.
Oh no! 'Twas the truth in her eye ever dawning
That made me love Mary, the Rose of Tralee."

Hmm, Keelin thought. So Flynn was quoting poetry to her now? She hid a small smile as she contemplated the line about the truth in her eye. Did Flynn want her to tell him about her gifts? She wasn't sure if she was ready to share that part of herself. Heck, she was still figuring it out for herself. Keelin wasn't certain if she was ready to tell people, well, regular people, about it.

Keelin scrounged in the cupboards until she found a lovely crystal vase for the flowers. She continued to hum to herself as she cut the flowers for the vase. It was a softly beautiful summer day and the windows were thrown open to catch the sea breezes. Keelin heard Ronan's barks grow closer as Fiona made her way up the path and into the cottage. Fiona stopped and exclaimed at the flowers as Ronan ran over to lick Keelin's feet.

"Well, well. That boy was raised right." Fiona fussed over the flowers and placed them on a small table by the open window. "These are just lovely."

"I know. He did good, I'll give him that." Keelin eyed the flowers warily.

Fiona turned and gave Keelin a hug. "It's intimidating to be pursued. And, really exciting too. Embrace it, enjoy it, and go with the flow. You'll have fun tonight. And, if my guess is correct, Flynn knows how to show a woman a good time." Fiona raised her eyebrows at her. Keelin laughed and touched her forehead to hers.

"I love you. I really do. I'm so glad that I came here and got to know you."

"You too, my dear. Now, let's get you ready for your date." Fiona bustled over to Keelin's room and pulled out the dress she had pressed for her. "You should wear your hair down, messy-like. Minimal jewelry I am thinking. Just skin, that gorgeous hair, and this dress. Much sexier of a statement. Do you have any flat sandals?"

"I do; I was going to wear these gold-threaded ones." Keelin pulled out a pair of flat, intricately woven gold sandals. They would allow her to walk around the boat without tripping on things or losing her balance.

"Perfect. Now, go shower. Don't forget to shave!" Fiona winked at her and Keelin laughed and shook her head. It seemed like the whole village wanted her to get laid tonight.

Keelin took her time in the shower, enjoying the steam and the warmth. Afterwards, she worked a natural lotion into her skin. It smelled faintly of vanilla and was a product that Fiona had helped her to create. She was proud of her work and smiled down at the small jar. Keelin figured she could probably sell it for a nice chunk of change back in Boston. She'd label it as all-natural herbal Irish products. The Boston Irish would eat it right up, she thought. Keelin realized that that was actually a fairly smart idea and she grabbed her iPad by the bed to jot down some notes. With a cute website and some expertly culled products, she suspected that she could have a neat little side business going. Thinking about becoming an entrepreneur kept her mind off of the nervousness of her date as she dried her hair and let it tumble in loose waves over her shoulders. Keelin scrunched her nose as she examined her face in the mirror. She decided on eyeliner to pop her eyes, a hint of blush for her cheeks, and kept her lips bare. The dress would be the showstopper tonight.

Keelin was just pulling the dress over her shoulders when she heard the knock at the door and Fiona's voice as she answered. She could have sworn she heard Fiona giggle like a girl and she rolled her eyes. Flynn could charm a rabid dog, she thought. Keelin felt a bolt of nervousness shoot through as she straightened in the mirror and examined herself one more time before she went into the living room. The red dress fulfilled the promise it had made in the store and accentuated all of her curves. Fiona had been right about Keelin leaving her hair down and messy. With just a light touch of makeup, messy hair, and the pretty gold sandals, Keelin looked sexy, carefree, and confident. She took a deep breath and went to meet Flynn.

Chapter Twenty

FLYNN'S EYES WIDENED as Keelin entered the room. She smiled shyly at him as he broke off his conversation with Fiona and traced his gaze over her. For once, the man had nothing to say.

"Hello, Flynn," Keelin said shyly as she gathered her wrap and a small bag. Flynn nodded at her as Fiona reached up and gave him a quick peck on the cheek. She picked up a book and wished them both a good evening before retiring into her bedroom. Flynn moved quickly around the table and stood before Keelin. She backed up a step, feeling a little unsteady. He had yet to say a word and it was making her stomach twinge.

Slowly, Keelin raised her eyes to Flynn's. The deep blue of his eyes bored into her own as he leaned down and nipped at her mouth. Gently, and ever so sweetly, he pressed his lips to hers. As he eased away, he smiled at her.

"You're gorgeous. If you wanted to punish me, this dress certainly does it. I'll barely be able to carry on a conversation tonight without wondering what you are wearing underneath it." Flynn raised an eyebrow at her.

Keelin's mouth went dry. She swallowed quickly. "Not much fits under this dress." She squeaked as he grabbed her to him and leaned to kiss her again. "Stop, stop. Come on, I want to see this boat of yours." Keelin glanced towards Fiona's door, certain the old woman was leaning against the door, listening.

Flynn groaned. Grabbing her hand, he dragged her from the room and out to a late-model truck that was parked in the drive. He stopped at her door and helped her to get in the truck, his hand sliding down her leg before he shut the door. Keelin took a shaky breath. If this was the type of tension between them, she doubted that they would make it through dinner.

"So, where do you dock this boat of yours?" Keelin asked as Flynn reversed and headed his truck in the other direction over the hills. The sun was just beginning to meander towards the horizon and a soft breeze blew the sea scents in through the window.

"On the other side of the cove. I have several docks there for a variety of my boats. It all depends on what I am fishing for that day."

"Oh, and what are you fishing for tonight?" Keelin said cheekily.

Flynn turned his powerful gaze on her. "The grand prize, of course."

Keelin gulped and didn't answer him. He chuckled as he wound his truck down the hill to the glistening shoreline below them. Several docks held a myriad variety of boats from small two-seaters to a large gleaming white yacht.

"The two-seater, I presume?" Keelin poked at his chest as he helped her out. Flynn laughed at her and held her hand as they walked down to the docks. It was surprisingly comfortable – the way her small hand felt in his rough palm. Little tendrils of heat seemed to curl up her arm from where they connected.

Flynn ushered her onto the dock that held the yacht. Though the boat was far larger than any of the others in his fleet, it was still manageable by one captain. Keelin saw nobody else on board as he guided her up the smooth gangplank to the first level of the boat. Warm teak wood panels ran the length of the boat and the floor. White leather cushions wrapped around the entire boat and various sitting spaces invited a visitor to lounge as wanted. At the front of the boat, a small table was set with flowers, small candles in mason jars, and a bottle of champagne icing in a bucket. Flynn motioned to the table.

"Would you like to pop the champagne while I get us on our way?" he asked as he finished untying the ropes that held the boat to the dock. He moved quickly to the steering wheel and a series of beeps sounded before the powerful hum of the engine trembled beneath the boat. Keelin watched him as he competently maneuvered the boat from the dock and switched their direction to facing outwards. It seemed like he did everything competently. If anything, this was a man who knew his own power. He must have been reading her thoughts because he sliced a glance at her and she took a quick sip of her champagne to cool the heat in her stomach.

"Would you like a glass?" she asked him quickly.

"Sure, a small one. I rarely drink if I am on the boat." Keelin moved from the table and over to stand by him at the helm. He accepted the glass and she stayed by his side, gazing out over the ocean as the sun moved to dip beneath the sea.

"It's so lovely. It's fun to be out on the water. I haven't gotten much of the water perspective since I've been here. I feel a little landlocked," Keelin said as she turned and gazed at the green hills that were growing smaller behind them.

"Would you like to drive?" Flynn asked her.

"Me? Yes! I'd love to." Keelin gigged as he switched spots with her and showed her the controls. She loved the feel of the steering wheel trembling under her hands. "Can we go fast?" Keelin shrieked as Flynn stepped behind her and punched the throttle forward. The momentum slammed her back into his hard body and he put his arms around her waist to steady her. She laughed as the wind tore her hair back and the waves pounded under the boat. It was so freeing to race across the water like this. She sighed as Flynn tapped the motor back down and the roar of the engine slowed.

"I have dinner planned and don't want it to go bad. Would you like to eat in the cove?" Flynn raised his eyebrows at her in a challenge.

"What? No. Seriously? Do you think it will be okay?" Keelin trembled a bit at the thought of the cove glowing blue.

"It's fine. You and I both have no problem going there if our intentions are pure." His eyes pierced hers. She stared up at his windswept hair, which framed his chiseled face. He leaned casually against the side of the boat, sexy in his untucked button-down and loose shorts. She wanted to unbutton his shirt with her teeth.

"Oh, they're pure," Keelin said quickly, though her thoughts were anything but. Flynn gave her a quick grin before he motored the boat into the cove. He stopped it in the deeper part of the water and threw an anchor to the bottom. Flynn cut the engines and the boat rocked lazily as small waves slapped against the sides. Keelin took a deep breath of the sea air and surveyed the cove from a new angle. The last of the sun's light cut across the cove's opening and shot rays across the middle of the cove while the surrounding hills stayed cloaked in darkness. Keelin turned when Flynn tugged at her hair. He pointed up into the sky where a full moon was beginning to rise as the sun set. Recognition slammed into her stomach as Keelin looked at the twin of the picture that Aislinn had given her. If there was ever a sign, she thought. A low hum began to fill her blood and Keelin decided to step into her own power.

"What's for dinner?" Keelin asked as she moved towards Flynn.

"I have cheese, fruits, salad, brown bread, and planned to sear some scallops in the small kitchen below." Flynn eyed her warily as she moved towards him. "Why?"

"Can it wait?" Keelin threaded her hands around his neck and leaned up to take a quick nip of his mouth. Just a taste.

"Oh, yeah. It can wait." Flynn molded his mouth to hers and she gasped as he swept her up and wrapped her legs around his waist. His lips continued a brutal assault on hers as he dipped his tongue deep in her mouth. Keelin felt warm tendrils of sensation shoot to her core as he walked her backwards. She huffed out a small laugh as he ran her into a chair. "Come on, let's go downstairs." Flynn set her down and made to pull her towards the opening for the stairs. Keelin eyed him and shook her head no. The pale moonlight washed over her as she grasped the hem of her dress. Flynn's eyes narrowed and became fiercely intent as she pulled the dress over her head and tossed it on the chair.

"Here." Keelin felt intoxicated. The soft moonlight caressed her curves and dips. Beneath her dress she wore no bra and only a small slip of a thong. Her shoes glittered on her feet and she laughed, tossed her hair back, and lifted her arms to the sky. "Definitely here."

"Oh, God. You're amazing." Flynn leapt to her and dragged her to the front of the boat, where he tossed some towels on a long, low lounge bed that dominated the front of the yacht. He turned and pulled her to him, running his hands over her curves. "I can't, I have to." Without saying anything more he dipped his head and captured her right breast in his mouth, his hands coming up to cradle both. Keelin gasped as sensations whiplashed through her and she moaned as he circled her nipples with his tongue.

"Oh, yes. Please, I love that." The gentle pressure of his mouth heightened as he sucked on her more deeply. Keelin ran her hands through his thick hair and tried not to melt into a puddle on the floor. She moaned as he ran one work-roughened hand down her waist and cupped her generous butt. Flynn slowly bumped her back to sit on the bed. He stood over her, panting as he reached to unbutton his shirt.

"Wait, let me." Keelin kneeled on the bed and smiled at him coyly. She was trying hard to keep her wits about her but sensations flooded her body just as much as emotions did. She bit her lip nervously as she unbuttoned the first button of his shirt and revealed his tanned chest. Testing him, she leaned forward and kissed his chest gently. At his soft intake of breath, she smiled against his skin, which smelled of the sun. Keelin quickly undid the rest of the buttons and followed the path that she had opened with her mouth. Flynn groaned as she reached his belt buckle, an obvious bulge straining against his pants. Keelin leaned in and kissed the small ridge of muscle that dipped into his pants. She laughed as he let out a low growl and she trailed her tongue across his stomach to kiss his other side. She squirmed as sensations flooded her. She ran her hands up his hard chest and locked gazes with him. "I want you. All of you."

"God, Keelin. I've wanted you since the moment I met you. Before then, even. I swear I've dreamt of you." It was the most revealing thing that Flynn had said to her and Keelin smiled at the warmth that spread through her. Holding his gaze, she undid his belt buckle and worked him free. Bending over, she took him deep into her mouth in one smooth motion. Flynn moaned as she taunted him with her mouth, owning her power, taking the reigns in their lovemaking. Giddy with her control, Keelin increased her movements until Flynn suddenly lifted her and threw her back on the bed.

"If you keep doing that we'll be over before we've started and I have a lot of plans for you, my love," Flynn said as he straddled her on the bed and pulled her thong down over her curvy legs. Keelin's heart clenched at him saying she was his love. She wondered if he meant it or if it was a simple term of endearment. She leaned her head back against the bed and stared up into the night sky, the stars beginning to wink out of the darkness as the pale full moon slowly began to rise. Keelin jerked as Flynn's rough hands slid up her legs. His mouth followed their path and he licked at her delicate inner thigh. Her legs twitched at the sensation and she tried not to squirm. Keelin glanced down to see Flynn's head between her legs. His gaze was predatory and he flashed her a wolfish grin.

"I want you to watch." Keelin's body spasmed as he dipped his mouth to her most sensitive of spots and caressed her with his tongue. She watched his dark head bob between her legs and his muscular arms came up to wrap around her legs and cup her butt. He lifted her and brought her closer to him. Keelin's head fell back against the bed and she writhed against his mouth as a suddenly bolt of heat whiplashed through her. Keelin screamed as he held her there while she bucked against his face, her sensitive core tingling at his touch. As the shudders racked her body, Keelin almost wept with gratitude. When she was spent, he softly lowered her to the lounge and moved so he lay between her legs and propped his arms around her. A pounding lust pulsed through Keelin and she wrapped her arms around his strong shoulders, pulling Flynn's full weight onto her. Hungrily, she kissed his mouth and tasted her sweetness on his lips.

"I need – I want –" Keelin gasped at him as she wrapped her legs around him and pulled his hard length closer to her core. "I want you."

"Ah, Keelin, my love. I want you too." Flynn sucked at her bottom lip as he thrust long and deep into her. Keelin gasped and moaned into his mouth as he filled her to her very core. Her muscles tightened around him instinctively and small fissures of sensations began to shoot through her as Flynn rocked slowly into her. Suddenly frantic, Keelin clawed his back as Flynn picked up his pace. Over and over he stroked her deep within as she held on to his shoulders. With one final shout, they shattered at the same time. She held her arms tight around Flynn and opened her eyes over his shoulder. A strange light seemed to emanate around them and Keelin jerked. Craning her neck, she saw the waters of the cove glowed a deep blue. Flynn whispered in her ear, "Are you okay?"

"What? Yes, I am just fine. Better than fine, really." Keelin watched as the light dimmed and disappeared as quickly as she had seen it. She recalled Fiona's words that the cove glowed in the presence of love. Shaky, and unsure of herself, she dipped her face into Flynn's neck.

"Um, I should have asked this. Are you on the pill?" Keelin shot a quick look at Flynn's face. It held a mixture of concern and regret.

"Yes, I am. No worries on that part." Keelin could have kicked herself. She had never been so impetuous before. What had come over her? Flynn gave her a small kiss and rolled so she was on top of him. She looked down into his gorgeous face and smiled. Flynn was what had come over her, that was what, she thought.

"I'm famished. Ready for dinner?" Keelin asked.

"Oh, I am. Just one more thing though," Flynn said.

"What's that?" Keelin asked, and shrieked as he pulled her to him, already ready for her again. "No, really?"

"Really."

Chapter Twenty-One

LATER, KEELIN USED the small restroom below deck. She had pulled her dress back on and examined her face in the mirror. Her skin looked dewy from a healthy, make that two healthy, rounds of sex, she thought. A small flush of color highlighted her cheeks and her brandy eyes looked bright. She smiled at herself. She looked happy for the first time in a long time. She was happy, she thought.

After refreshing herself, Keelin came upstairs to the scent of scallops. Flynn must have seared them while she was using the bathroom. The plate was set with a small board of cheeses, fruits, and brown bread. Small bowls held salads and he plated the scallops on pretty stoneware dishes. A bottle of white wine chilled in the bucket.

"Wine?"

"Yes, I'd love some." Suddenly shy, Keelin blushed as he moved towards her with a glass. Flynn laughed at her and gave her a small kiss.

"No need to blush now, my love. I've seen every part of you." Keelin groaned as he laughed at her. There it was again, the love word. She'd have to pay attention and see how often he used it around other people or if it was just with her.

They settled around the table and soon Flynn began to her regale her with his boyhood tales of growing up in the hills. He told her of his love for dogs and how it had grown into an avid hobby of his. Keelin told him what life was like growing up in Boston – a single kid with a single mom. His childhood seemed much richer than hers. She said as much as she let the butter and scallops melt on her tongue.

"It seems like the perfect childhood."

"I have no complaints. I'm not sure how well I would have done in a city. A boy needs the hills to roam and learn. Luckily, my parents indulged me and allowed me to develop a variety of interests. Hence the fishing, the restaurants, the dogs. I have a hard time focusing on just one job."

"Well, that is very admirable of you. Tell me about your restaurants." Keelin sipped her wine and listened as his eyes lit up and he talked about creating jobs in small villages that needed the tourist attractions. She admired how committed he was not only to his businesses, but also to the struggling Irish economy. "How do you juggle so many businesses?"

"I have managers that I trust at each place. They all own a percentage of the restaurant so they are just as invested in it as I am." Flynn gestured with his fork as he speared another scallop.

"That's smart. I have to say, you really are a kind man. I see how you are with your dog, and now with your employees. Fiona loves you."

"And I her." Flynn nodded at Keelin as he broke off a crust of brown bread.

"Does the healing thing freak you out?" Keelin asked casually as she popped a piece of cheese into her mouth.

"Why would it? People have been using herbs for natural remedies for centuries. It isn't that uncommon." Flynn dismissed their powers easily, Keelin thought.

"No, I mean, well of course that. But you know, the whole other stuff." Keelin wasn't sure how to say it.

"What, the rumors that she is a witch? That woman is no more a witch than my dog is." Flynn laughed as he got up to clear their dishes and headed below deck.

Keelin was stunned. She sat there and stared at the darkness of the cove. He didn't know. Fiona had never told him of her ability to heal with her hands. Heat flushed through her. She didn't know if she should tell him. She was scared to. What if he would hate her?

"You know all of that stuff is just nonsense. And people who subscribe to that line of thought are just nuts," Flynn said as he came upstairs with small slices of cheesecake on plates. "Don't worry, I would never believe anything so horrible about Fiona."

Keelin nodded and quietly took a gulp of her wine. She trembled. She couldn't tell him. He would think she was a freak. Could she have a relationship with Flynn and hide this from him? She looked at him as he smiled and proudly presented her with the cheesecake. Oh, yes. She wanted this. She wanted a chance with him. Deciding to keep her mouth closed, she took a quick bite of the cheesecake and groaned as the sweetness exploded onto her tongue.

"This is amazing."

"I know. Isn't it? This old woman in town who looks like a troll makes the most delicate of desserts. I use her to supply all of my restaurants with baked goods. It tastes like heaven."

Keelin devoured her piece along with her glass of wine. She wondered if tonight would be all she would get with Flynn before he found out about her true identity. It would come out at some point. Suddenly desperate, she jumped up.

"You haven't shown me the downstairs yet, Flynn." Keelin raised an eyebrow at him and cocked her hip. Flynn's plate clattered to the table and he jumped up to wrap his arms around her waist. His lips tasted of cheesecake and she smiled against them as he led her downstairs. She didn't want to look at the cove this time.

Chapter Twenty-Two

LATER THAT NIGHT, Flynn parked in her drive. He leaned over and pressed a gentle kiss to her lips before getting out and rounding the hood of the car. Flynn opened the door and helped her down. He held her hand lightly as he led her to the door.

"I'd ask to spend the night with you but I don't want to shock Fiona," Flynn said as he rested his forehead on hers. Keelin felt warmth pool through her as her heart clenched a bit and trembled.

"Someday, maybe."

"I'd like to take you out again." Flynn laid a whisper of a kiss on her lips.

"Yes, I had fun." Flynn laughed at her as she blushed at the thought of the fun they'd had.

"I'll stop by to see you the day after tomorrow. We can go for a walk in the hills?"

Keelin nodded. She had to see him again. She didn't want him to go. Heat pulsed through her at every point his body came into contact with hers.

"Yes, Monday. I'll plan for it." She turned and slipped in the door only to hear his quiet words.

"Goodnight, my love."

Chapter Twenty-Three

THE NEXT DAY, Keelin kept reviewing the date in her mind. She was unaccountably nervous. All morning, she had replayed his words to herself. Was "my love" the same as "loving" someone? Was it just a term of endearment? Her heart clenched at the thought of loving him. The view of the cove's glowing water haunted her.

Fiona bustled in from the outside, bringing in sunshine and a rambunctious puppy. Keelin smiled as Ronan raced to her and wiggled at her feet, begging for a scratch.

"Keelin! How was your date last night?" Fiona asked breathlessly. She hung up her coat on the hook by the door and moved to the table with the bag of herbs that she had collected that morning. Keelin blushed as she thought about how to answer the question. "Ah, so he's a fine lover then," Fiona said as she caught the blush on Keelin's face.

Keelin sighed. "He's wonderful. Everything about him. He's a good employer, concerned about the economy, loves dogs, honest, and hardworking. Not to mention gorgeous." Keelin kicked at the table leg.

"So, why aren't you happy?" Fiona stopped sorting her herbs and gave her full attention to Keelin.

"I just...I don't know. I couldn't tell him about our power." She looked at Fiona nervously. "How did you tell Grandpa?"

"Well, honey, I was honest with him. If you can't show the person you love all the corners of your soul, do they really love you or just an image of you? Why would you want to live like that? Forever hiding a secret?"

"I don't know. I really don't. I guess I'm not used to discussing this and I have seen how it has led to destruction in my past relationships. I'm scared. I really think that I have a thing here with Flynn. The cove glowed last night."

"Ahhh." Fiona rushed around the table and gave Keelin a small hug. "So, it is love. On both parts. You have to tell him, Keelin."

"I know. I know. I will. We are going hiking tomorrow. Maybe I will tell him then."

Chapter Twenty-Four

RESTLESS, KEELIN DECIDED to take a drive into the village to tell Cait about Flynn's boat. And, well, just to talk to someone with similar issues to hers. Keelin pulled up to the pub and stretched, feeling twinges in muscles that she hadn't felt in a long time. Even though she was nervous, it was almost impossible to keep the smile off of her face. An evening of being lapped up like she was the best dessert on the table would do that, Keelin thought, and swung through the door of the pub.

"Well, I'm not one of those fancy women that you take up with, am I now?" Cait shouted at Shane. Her heated tone had Keelin stopping in her tracks.

Cait and Shane faced each other across the room, mere inches apart, both of their chests heaving.

"Whoo, boy," Keelin whispered under her breath, and didn't move.

"Who said that I want one of those fancy women?" Shane countered.

"It's plain as all can see, isn't it? Nothing but the richest for Shane," Cait said.

"I don't know where this is coming from, Cait. You're being crazy," Shane said, and ran his hands through his hair in frustration.

"Oh, crazy is it? Well, then you can just take yourself right out of my pub. Wouldn't want you associating with a mad woman, now," Cait sputtered at Shane.

Keelin's mouth dropped open as Shane wrenched Cait to his chest and captured her lips in a smoldering kiss before shoving her away from him.

"You're crazy. You drive me crazy. This is all crazy," Shane muttered to himself. Seeing Keelin, he threw his hands up in the air and breezed past her out of the door. Keelin turned to watch him go and then looked back to Cait, her eyebrow raised.

Cait stood with her hand to her lips, her face slack with a mixture of shock and lust. Keelin walked over and waved her hand in front of Cait's face.

"Hello…earth to Cait," Keelin said.

Cait's eyes snapped to hers. "Sorry about that."

"Oh, don't be. Really, it was most entertaining," Keelin said and laughed down at Cait. Cait moved behind the bar and poured them both a cider without asking. Keelin settled onto a stool and studied her friend's flushed cheeks.

"So, want to tell me about that?" Keelin asked.

"Nope, not in the slightest. I can see it all over you that you have way more exciting news. So, dish." Cait gestured with her cider.

Keelin eyed her for a moment. "Okay, I'll give you a free pass. For now. And only because, yes, I have the best story for you."

Keelin all but glowed as she filled Cait in on her night.

"Three times? Three!" Cait squealed at the end of it and Keelin laughed.

"Three," she said.

"So, when do you see him next?" Cait asked.

"Tomorrow: we are going hiking. I'm nervous," Keelin admitted.

"Because you haven't told him about yourself, have you?" Cait asked, reading Keelin's mind.

"I haven't. I...he just seems so resistant to the concept. How do I even begin?" Keelin asked as she tore apart a bar napkin.

"I don't know. I really don't. But all I can say is...the sooner, the better. You don't want to get too far along with him and have him find out. He'll never forgive you," Cait said ominously.

Keelin finished her cider and mulled it over. Cait was right. She'd just have to do it on the hike tomorrow. Worst-case scenario, he'd run screaming over the hills to get away from her. Keelin could only hope that it was far less dramatic than that.

Chapter Twenty-Five

FIONA HELPED KEELIN to pack her hiking bag the next day. The old woman fussed nervously over her.

"I'm fine," Keelin said.

"I know, I know. I just…never mind," Fiona said as a knock on the door interrupted them.

"Coming!" Keelin yelled out, and snagged her small pack for a day hike. "I shouldn't be too late."

"Good luck, my dear girl. Remember, true love sees all."

Keelin nodded and stepped into the sunshine and the warmth of Flynn's smile. He scooped her up immediately and caressed her lips with his. Startled, Keelin let out a laugh as she sunk into his mouth. He tasted elemental – all manly and earthy. On a small moan, she stopped herself and leaned back to look into his deep blue eyes.

"Morning, handsome." Keelin smiled up at him and tried not to sink into his eyes. Oh, she was for sure a goner, she thought as her heart tripped a bit and seemed to fall off a ledge into her stomach.

"Hey, beautiful. I thought about you all night. I couldn't wait to see you again today." Flynn smiled openly and easily at her as he took her hand and led her down a path. Keelin's heart clenched a bit. She wanted to fall into this easy rhythm with him. She didn't want there to be secrets. How would she bring the subject up?

They followed a path over the hills and winding around the other side of the cove. The sun was retreating behind one of Ireland's famous mists, yet it was still warm enough for a hike. Keelin realized that she was able to identify many of the plants and flowers thanks to Fiona's tutelage. They reached the base of a path that led up a sharp cliff. Though the ascent didn't look to carry on for that long, the path was severe.

Flynn stopped her at the base. "Up for a climb? It is tough but only for a small bit. The view is worth the climb."

"Absolutely. I would love to see the view."

"Why don't you go first? That way I can catch you if you slide," Flynn joked at her.

"Sure, you just want to look at my butt," Keelin teased as she poked a finger into the muscles of his hard stomach. He grabbed her hand and pulled her to him, trailing his hands down to cup her bottom.

"Mmm, I certainly do love it. Maybe we should stop here and rest for a bit." Flynn wiggled his eyebrows at her and pulled until she was locked against the hard length of him. Heat shot straight to her core.

"Oh no, this one is for the top. Last one up owes the other a massage!" Keelin laughed at him and turned tail to run up the path. She heard his chuckle behind her but didn't look back. Soon she her breath came out in heavy puffs as she navigated the rocky terrain. Rocks slipped out from under her feet as she heaved herself over sharp rock piles, and she gasped as her foot slipped and caught the sharp edge of a stick. Rolling her eyes, Keelin told herself to slow down. This was a dangerous path and she needed to be careful.

"Keelin!" Flynn's shout broke her thoughts and she turned to see him fall from the ledge below her.

Panic raced through Keelin as she screamed for Flynn. Her heart pounding, she turned to race down the ledge and realized it was too steep to do so. She would have to back down as a rock climber would. Trying to hurry and calling Flynn's name repeatedly, Keelin eased herself painstakingly down the path.

"Flynn. Please, Flynn, answer me. Flynn!" She reached level ground and raced to where Flynn was crumpled over his leg. Her heart slammed into her chest and she forced herself to take deep breaths as she saw a pool of blood rapidly flowing from him. Flynn groaned and leaned backwards. His face was ashen and quickly turning to white.

"Help. Run. It's bad. Really bad. Please. Call for help," Flynn gasped out.

"Here, let me look." Keelin kneeled at his side and tried not to wince at the rapid flow of blood. Flynn's hands were covering a large wound in his leg. He applied pressure and was trying to stop the flow of blood but it squirted from beneath his hands. Keelin ripped his pants open and discovered the cause of the blood. A compound fracture had caused his bone to rip through his thigh. And, judging from the flow of blood, he had ripped his femoral artery. Keelin knew that death would come soon without a tourniquet and immediate medical aid.

"Okay, Flynn, don't look. Just keep the pressure on. I am going to make a tourniquet." Keelin stripped off her shirt and ripped it into several strips before she laid it underneath his leg and told him to brace himself. She looked around for a few sticks. Finding some near, she placed one in his mouth and the other in the shirt to tighten it.

"This is going to hurt. Just hang on." Flynn nodded at her and closed his eyes. His color was fading fast. Keelin quickly tied the tourniquet and pulled it as tight as she could. She could feel the tension in Flynn as he clenched his jaw around the stick. The gray dregs of panic threatened to cloud her head and Keelin tried to breathe. What now? Keelin pulled Flynn's hands from the wound and saw that the tourniquet had done little to stem the flow of blood. If she didn't save him now, he would die.

Keelin reached for her pack. Inside was her necklace. Grace O'Malley's necklace, she reminded herself. She had packed it this morning for some odd reason and now she knew why. She placed it over her head and the stone warmed itself between her breasts, a low hum throbbing through her skin. Flynn eyes tracked her through his narrowed eyelids.

Keelin hiccupped a sob out as she pressed her hands to Flynn's leg. She watched as the blood squirted between her fingers and her mind whirled. She couldn't breathe – couldn't think. Could she do this? Could she heal someone – not just someone – but the man she loved? She wanted to scream. She wasn't prepared for this. Fiona hadn't taught her how to handle emergencies. What if she made it worse? With a quick glance at Flynn's pale face, Keelin realized there wasn't much opportunity for it to get any worse. He was close to death.

Keelin took one of her hands, slick with blood, and wrapped it around her amulet. Instantly, her mind cleared and the stone grew hot in her hand. Keelin closed her eyes and placed her hands on Flynn's leg. She whispered a short prayer of love. A soft white ball of light formed in her mind's eye. She imagined the ball of light traveling through her mind and down into her heart. From her heart, she poured all of her love into the ball of light and it began to pulse with a dull pink light. Taking her love, her heart, she allowed the ball of light to run through her arms and into her hands. In her mind, she could see the dull edges of death creeping through Flynn's veins towards the beautiful blue light of his soul.

Suddenly furious, Keelin forced her light into Flynn's leg and slammed it in front of the dark light creeping towards his heart. She gasped as pain shot through her. Determined to hold on, she fought the dull blackness and started to build a wall around it with her white light. Over and over, she pushed the sticky black stain further from his leg, creating building blocks along the way. Her entire body shook with the effort, and sweat dripped in a stream down her back. Tears, unbeknownst to her, ran down her face and into his wound. Over and over, Keelin prayed for her light to rebuild his artery and to knit the bone in his leg. Her strength began to fade and she shook with the effort of holding on until she was certain the dark light was gone. In one final push, her amulet burned to her chest, and with a loud snap, her light eradicated the darkness in his leg.

Flynn jumped to his feet. "What the hell was that?" His fury blasted her.

Shocked, Keelin stared at his angry face and slid into the darkness.

Chapter Twenty-Six

A GRAY HAZE shrouded her vision. Keelin could barely make out shapes or colors. She was so confused. Where was she? Flynn? Was Flynn okay? Frantically, she tried to turn her head and search for him.

Keelin realized she was no longer on the trail. She could vaguely make out the familiar surroundings of her bedroom. She squinted as the shapes became clearer. Flynn stood over her bed. His strong shoulders were hunched and his face was tense. He wiped sweat from his brow and laid a hand on the bed. Fiona stood next to him and she held a small jar in her hands. Keelin moved closer.

"Flynn. You're okay. I'm so glad." Keelin reached out to Flynn and watched her hand go through him. Keelin gasped as she looked down and saw herself lying on the bed. Her eyes were closed and her face was bone white and devoid of emotion. Panic slammed into her and she let

219

out a guttural scream that shook her soul. "No. Flynn. Fiona. Help me!"

"They can't hear you."

Keelin whipped her head around to see a woman standing in the corner. She was dressed oddly, as though she were in a play from the 1600s.

"Please, please help me. What is happening?" Keelin ran to her and grabbed her arm. The woman smiled at her gently and reached up to trace her face with her hand.

"My blood. The daughter of my daughters. My love." Her warm brandy eyes drank in Keelin's face.

"Grace? Grace O'Malley? Oh my God. Am I dead? Am I dreaming?"

"You're neither. You're in the veil between both, which is why I can reach you."

"What happened?" Keelin looked back at herself on the bed. It was oddly disorientating to see herself lying there, unresponsive. Fiona had pulled the sheet down and rubbed some of the ointment into her mouth and onto her chest. Keelin watched as she placed her hands over her heart. She felt a small prick of warmth in her chest and Grace's image became watery.

"You saved Flynn. But you forgot to direct the pain from you. Instead, you took it into your heart."

Keelin gasped at Grace's words. Fiona had warned her of this. She wouldn't survive this. Keelin hung her head and began to weep. Her time on this earth was over and her love for Flynn unrealized. Her body began to tremble as waves of sadness rocked through her. She had wanted, no, needed, more time.

"My dear girl. Do you love him?"

Keelin nodded. Words escaped her.

"Love is the strongest of medicines. Watch as Fiona works on you. You can see her love pouring into you. You'll be given another chance. But only if you honor your love for Flynn. Take him to the cove and show him everything. Bare your soul or lose your chance at life."

Keelin felt the warmth begin to spread through her. Hope leaped in her stomach. Light began to fill her as she raised her eyes to Grace's — a twin of her own. "And if I can't tell him?"

"You'll live. But as a shell of yourself, and true happiness will forever escape you. Deny who you are and life isn't worth living." Grace leaned over and placed a gentle kiss on her brow. She smoothed her hair and began to fade. Keelin looked from her to Fiona and Flynn, desperately huddled over the bed. "Goodbye, my child. I will wait for you."

Keelin looked back at her and her vision seemed to fragment and snap as heat shot through her. She shrieked out a breath and realized that Flynn and Fiona now stood over her. Keelin blinked rapidly and tried to speak. Her mouth was dry and she coughed.

"Oh, oh, Keelin. There you are. I was so worried. Shh. Don't talk. Don't say anything. Let me get you some ice chips." Fiona shuddered and wiped tears from her eyes. She ran to grab a glass of ice chips.

Unable to speak, Keelin raised her gaze to Flynn. Joy rushed through her as she realized that she had saved his life. His face was tense and his eyes were shuttered. He clenched his hands over and over around a small stick he held in his palms. Slowly, he met her eyes. She looked at him and offered him a small smile. Flynn looked at her and shook his head. He turned and stormed from the room, slamming the front door to the cottage on the way out.

Keelin's heart shattered. She began to weep. Her whole body ached to scream and cry but she simply had no energy. Fiona rushed in and hovered over her.

"Shh, shh, my love. Shh. We'll fix this. We will." Fiona spooned ice chips into Keelin's mouth. The cool slide of the ice cube did little to soothe the heat of the panic that gripped her.

"I didn't get a chance to tell him about me. He saw it first," Keelin gasped out. She shook as the tears coursed over her face.

"Shh. I know. He told me. It will be okay. Just hush. You need to get your strength back first. We'll figure this out. If Flynn is the man that I think he is then he will accept you for you. Let me get some of my broth. I need to make sure you get some strength back." Fiona hurried from the room, clucking her tongue. Keelin rolled to her side and stared blankly at the room. Two paws and a small head popped up on the side of the bed. Ronan tilted his head at her quizzically and then leaned in to lick her tears. She smiled at him and patted the bed. He quickly jumped up and nuzzled into her, whimpering softly. His kindness made the tears come faster and he whined softly as he continued to lick her face.

"Good boy, Ronan. Good boy." She ran her hand down his soft fur and was grateful for his comfort. Fiona rushed back into the room with a steaming teapot and poured water into a bowl full of herbs.

"This is my special blend. You must drink it all." She leaned over to help Keelin sit up and tucked pillows behind her. Keelin could barely lift her arms so Fiona held the bowl to her lips. Keelin blew on the hot mixture and, suddenly ravenous, she took large sips of the broth, not caring if she burned her tongue. She was so happy to feel anything – even if it was pain. She didn't want to be back in that gray place where everything was numb.

"I saw Grace," Keelin said as she felt the medicine of the broth slowly work through her body. Energy spikes started to twitch in her arms and legs and she began to slowly wiggle her fingers and toes.

"You…you saw Grace? When?" Fiona stopped spooning her the broth and stared at her. Keelin saw concern flash across her weathered cheeks.

"I was in the veil. I wasn't here but I wasn't there either. I could see you and Flynn and…and…myself. On the bed. She was in the corner and spoke to me."

"Oh my. Oh, Keelin. How scary. And, what an incredible gift." Fiona smoothed the hair from Keelin's brow and smiled at her. "She gave you back to me, didn't she?"

"Yes. On the contingency that I give Flynn my whole soul or live a life of unhappiness." Keelin started as Fiona huffed out a small laugh.

"Oh, I love the spunk of that woman. I'd heard she always drove a hard bargain."

"Flynn, he hates me. He was disgusted by me." Tears threatened to well up in Keelin's eyes again and she hurriedly took another sip of the broth.

"He most certainly does not. You should have seen that man. I've never seen anyone run across the hills like that. He carried you over his shoulder, shouting the whole way, while he ran like the wind." Fiona smoothed the sheets around Keelin.

"Well, I know he doesn't want me to die but that doesn't mean he isn't disgusted by what I am."

Fiona opened her mouth to speak and stopped. She took the empty bowl from Keelin's hands.

"I guess that is for you to find out, isn't it?" Fiona said gently. Annoyance whipped through Keelin. She wanted Fiona to tell her that Flynn loved her and that he would do anything for her. She heaved a big sigh as she realized that those were questions that only she could answer for herself.

"Okay. I will."

"You're a good girl. I love you so much. Later, you'll have to tell me about today. For now, you must sleep. Doctor's orders. I'll leave Ronan with you."

Keelin smiled at her and grasped the old woman's hand between her own. "Thank you for saving me. I love you too." Fiona smiled and cleared the dishes before she pulled the shades and closed the door to the room quietly. She curled herself around Ronan's warm body and immediately fell into the deep sleep of sheer exhaustion.

Chapter Twenty-Seven

SHARP HUNGER PAINS woke Keelin. She groaned and rolled over, dreaming of French toast. She sat up quickly as the events of the day before washed over her. It all felt like a weird dream. Keelin gingerly reached out her arms and then swung her legs off of the bed. Though she was a little unsteady when she stood, she felt good. She felt alive, she reminded herself. Keelin shuddered in a breath as she realized how close she had come to dying.

She stumbled into the bathroom and flicked the light on. She met her eyes in the mirror. Her face looked different. It looked older somehow. Not in age lines, but in wisdom. She imagined it was how a soldier's face looked after a battle. There seemed to be a new power to her — a knowledge — that came from being so close to the edge. Everything had shifted for her yesterday. Keelin had to decide what that would mean for her. Would the pain of this experience casually fade with time or would the lessons learned change her very core? She suspected it was the latter of the two. She already felt like a different person.

Keelin pulled a demure one-piece bathing suit on and threw a loose dress over her head. From habit, she braided her hair as she walked into the kitchen to find Fiona bustling over the stove. She started when Keelin padded silently behind her and laid a kiss on her cheek.

"Oh! You're up. Let me look at you." Fiona turned and held Keelin's face in her hands and looked deep into her eyes. Keelin smiled at the old woman, drinking in all of the age lines and wisdom her face held. "You look better. You've changed, haven't you?" Fiona gestured to the table and Keelin gratefully sat in front of a plate that held warm blueberry scones and fresh cream.

"Mm, this looks delicious." Keelin nodded at Fiona with her mouth full as she placed a rasher of bacon by her plate. "Yes, I feel like I've changed. I don't know how yet. But it seems like I have a choice to make. Either I embrace everything I am or lose everything I have."

Fiona settled onto the stool across from Keelin and sipped her tea. She paused for a moment before she spoke. "I don't know if it is all or nothing like you think. But I do know that when you heal someone like that and you take it into you, you'll forever know your true power as a healer. You've pushed yourself as far as you can go. Because of that, your limits are now defined. In some respects, this makes you a far better and more efficient healer."

"That makes sense. I wasn't even thinking about what I was doing. I was so distraught that I just went into autopilot. It was a stupid move."

"Why did you allow that energy into your body? Why didn't you send it away? Tell me what happened."

Keelin filled Fiona in on the whole scenario up until when Flynn's leg had healed and he had stared at her with such anger. A small sob caught in her throat and her hand shook as she took a quick sip of her tea. "He…he hated me, Fiona. His face was so full of anger. It wasn't even gratitude. I was so startled that I never finished the healing session because I swear my heart just broke when I saw his face." Keelin shredded the rest of the scone on her plate, nervously picking the bits into small crumbs.

"So you didn't get a chance to talk to him before he hurt himself?" Fiona asked, and slid a new scone onto Keelin's plate.

"I was going to. We were just having fun and I was going to tell him at the top of the climb. It is kind of a weird thing to talk about when you are hiking and not looking at each other face to face."

"He doesn't hate you. But you do need to make this right with him," Fiona said.

"Why do I need to make it right? Why do I have to be ashamed of what I am?" Keelin demanded furiously. "I saved his damn life and he walked away. You healed me and he took one look to make sure that I was alive and stormed out the door. I'm so furious with him that I don't even know if I want to see him!" She slammed her mug on the table and Ronan whined softly from under her chair. Keelin slipped her hand down and rubbed his silky ears between her fingers.

"I understand that you are hurt. Of course you are hurt. But, you also have to see it from his side. He views this as a betrayal. You have this whole other life that you didn't tell him about. And, no, you should never be ashamed of what you are. I'm not suggesting you apologize to him for that. I suggest you apologize for not sharing your whole self with him."

"Hmpf. Like I'll even get to see him anytime soon," Keelin said morosely.

"Don't give him a choice. Go to the cove. Don't forget that you met Grace. Which, by the way, I plan to pick your head about later. Go to the cove, Keelin. You need to finish this one way or the other." Fiona got up and handed her a pen and paper. "Tie a note to Ronan's collar. He'll know what to do."

Keelin stared at the small notepad for a moment. She wasn't entirely sure what to say. What would be convincing enough to have him meet her there?

"It is said that when a person saves another's life – that they are forever indebted to that person. I ask of you a favor. Meet me at the cove. I will wait until sundown."

Keelin tied the note up and wrapped it around Ronan's collar. Fiona packed her a bag of food and wine and gave her a long hug. Keelin leaned into her and smelled her neck, which smelled faintly of lavender and moss. Warmth surrounded them as they hugged.

"Thank you for my life. I will love you always," Keelin whispered to her. Fiona nodded against her and held her tight.

"You are my blood." Fiona reached up and slipped Grace's amulet around Keelin's neck. "You forgot this."

"Thank you, I thought it was gone!" Keelin looked down at the stone nestled on her chest.

"No, you still had it on when Flynn carried you here. It was covered in his blood," Fiona said meaningfully, and ushered her out the door.

Keelin's stomach felt like it was tied in knots. She glanced down at Ronan and then up to the hills. Flynn's dog sat up on the ridge.

"Ronan, go to Flynn." She whistled and Teagan ran down to collect Ronan. "Go home, go on now." She waited as she watched the two dogs race up the hill and out of sight. Taking a deep breath, Keelin turned to the cove, her future at its shores.

Chapter Twenty-Eight

A̶T THE BASE of the path to the cove, Keelin stopped. Here was where she would traditionally say a small prayer and give an offering. Bending over, she unstrapped her sandals and kicked them aside. Keelin walked briskly to the edge of the water and let the waves lap over her feet. Reaching into her pack, she pulled out a small knife. Without hesitation, she used the sharp blade to slice a small cut into her palm. Clenching her fist, she held her hand over the water. A small rivulet of blood squeezed from the cut in her hand. She watched, hypnotized, as the blood hit the water in small drops of red, quickly dissipating.

"Yesterday, I almost gave my life because I refused to fully accept myself. I come here today to step into my birthright. I offer my blood to the cove, as a descendent of Grace O'Malley, as a promise to both myself and to her. I promise to protect the cove and I promise to never stand ashamed of what I am." Keelin squeezed extra hard and a long rivulet of blood dripped into the cove. A crack like a lightening bolt hit the water and for an instant it glowed a bright white. Keelin felt the hair on the back of her neck stand up. She knew Flynn was behind her.

Slowly, she turned, her hand still bloody.

Flynn stood at the end of the path, his hands tucked loosely into his pants pockets. A chambray shirt hung loose on him and dark circles marred his eyes. His shoulders were hunched. He eyed her, clearly on guard.

Keelin felt her heart clench. She slowly walked to him, her bleeding hand in front of her.

"Jesus, Keelin. What did you do?" Flynn automatically stepped forward to take her hand. She stepped back quickly and evaded his reach.

"No. Watch." Flynn eyed her warily as she opened her palm to reveal the long slice across her skin. She heard his small intake of breath as he realized that she had done this to herself. Keelin met his eyes. She looked down at her bloody hand and covered it with her other. She closed her eyes briefly and focused on the pain and sent her light down to heal it. The amulet warmed against her chest. Feeling the light gather, she sent the ball of pain into a small bush nearby. Slowly, Keelin opened her eyes to look at Flynn. She held both palms open, her pretty skin free of cuts. Flynn took a step back, anger on his face.

"I won't deal with witches, Keelin. I'm sorry, but I just won't," Flynn said angrily. He crossed his arms in front of his chest, a storm of emotions in his eyes.

"This is me, Flynn. This is all of me. I can heal people with my hands. I'm not a witch. I'm a descendent of Grace O'Malley." Keelin spoke quietly but proudly. The amulet at her neck began to grow warmer.

"I don't understand. I mean, I know that Fiona heals people with herbs and whatnot, but this? This hand stuff? It's crazy." Flynn dragged a hand through his hair.

"It is crazy. I wish that I could explain it to you any more than I can understand it myself. I don't know how it works, I just know that I can do it. I've run from this gift my entire life and it wasn't until I came here that I realized running was futile. This is me. All of me." Keelin stared at him as her stomach turned. "I'm…I'm sorry that I didn't tell you. I am just getting used to it myself. And, I was scared you would hate me. Which you do anyway," she said morosely as she put her hands down by her sides.

"I don't…I don't hate you. But, Jesus, Keelin. I was dying. I felt it! Blood was everywhere! And I sat there and watched you knit my bone back together. You put my artery back together! I could walk. It was terrifying! I didn't even know who you were at that point or what was happening. And then all of a sudden, you're dying on me!" Flynn was shouting at this point and pacing the beach. His shouts echoed off the rocky walls of the cove. Anger flashed through Keelin. Vaguely, Keelin registered a small rumble and saw the waves beginning to pick up.

"Well, I'm just so sorry. Was I supposed to leave you there to die? I'm sorry that you can't handle this but maybe you could, oh I don't know, thank me for saving your stubborn life? Had you not been so damn angry at me I would have been able to complete the healing and send the energy elsewhere. Instead I took it into me because you…you broke my heart." On a sob, Keelin turned and ran from Flynn. She was stupid to come here with him. He would never accept her for what she was.

Keelin let out a whoosh of breath as she was tackled from behind and flipped over. "Ooof!" she shrieked out as she landed on top of Flynn. He had turned to cushion her from the fall. Quickly, he rolled and pinned her underneath him.

"What do you mean that I broke your heart?" Flynn demanded.

"Nothing. I meant nothing. You are just a big jerk and I don't need someone like that in my life." Keelin avoided his eyes and stuck her chin out. Small fissures of heat curled through her where their bodies touched and she tried not to squirm under him. Keelin gasped as a huge wave crashed over them and shocked their bodies. Flynn sputtered out salt water and stared, aghast, at the beach. The shoreline was too far for a wave to have hit them.

"What the heck was that?" Flynn demanded. "Did you do that?"

"Of course I didn't do that, you punk. I told you that I'm not a witch. The cove is mad at me is all. Probably you too. You should go," Keelin said spitefully. Another wave slammed into them both and they rolled from the impact. "Damn it. Fine!" Keelin shouted as she found herself pinned under Flynn again, soaking wet, her body wide awake.

"You broke my heart because I love you. I have no idea how or when but I do. And when you stared at me like…like I was some kind of monster I froze and forgot to heal the way that I was taught by Fiona. No big deal. It's fine. I can get over this. But I refuse to apologize for what I am. If there is anything that I have learned from this it is that you have to love me for me or not at all," Keelin spit out, and then stuck her chin in the air. Her heart was pounding against her chest and she shivered at the heat that was building in her most sensitive of spots.

"Damn it, Keelin. You died. I watched you die. I just, it was too much. I couldn't wrap my head around what happened and then you just…you died. I was terrified." Flynn brought his forehead to hers. Keelin's heart hiccupped. Hope slid into her stomach.

"You left me. I came to and you just left," Keelin whispered. She felt tears prick her eyes. "You hurt me," she whispered.

"I'm sorry. I'm so sorry. I shouldn't have left. I didn't sleep at all last night. I planned to come today to apologize. It doesn't matter what you are, Keelin. You're heart is pure as gold. So is Fiona's. I could never look at what the both of you are and hate you. I love you. All of you. Every last stubborn bit." Flynn raised his eyes to hers as Keelin felt her whole body flare with a flash of heat.

"You do? You really do?" Keelin felt the heat rush over her in a wave and she began to cry thick, fat tears, and wrapped her arms around his broad shoulders.

"Yes, you difficult, strong, beautiful woman. I fell for you the moment that I saw you. I want you as much as I want my next breath." Flynn captured her mouth with his and swallowed Keelin's sobs. Her body shuddered with emotion as her heart sang. She heard a loud crack and pulled back to stare at the cove. It glowed a brilliant blue and a small flash of white light beamed from a cave far out in the rocky wall of the cove. Almost indecipherable from the other rocks, Keelin would never have seen the small tunnel.

"Flynn! Look!" He turned and she felt his body go rigid at the image of the gently pulsing light that emanated from the cove and the cave.

"What…what is it?" Flynn said warily. He shifted to protect her.

"No, it's okay. It's said that the cove glows in the presence of true love. And, that tunnel must be where the chalice is. The cove is showing us her secrets. It trusts us." Keelin smiled at the cove and silently thanked Grace for the gift. She would be sure to honor it.

Flynn shook his head ruefully as the glow in the water subsided. He smiled a crooked smile down at her and Keelin's eyes pricked at how close she had come to losing this man.

"So, are our kids going be witches too?"

Keelin laughed at him and smacked him on the arm before capturing his mouth in a kiss. Slowly, they lost themselves in each other. Excited barks broke through the fog around them and they were bombarded with puppy licks. Keelin giggled and Flynn helped her to her feet. Together, they pet their dogs and wrapped their arms around each other as they began the hike up out of the cove. Keelin glanced back to see the sun dipping on the horizon and a pale sliver of moon beginning to shine in the sky. She nodded silently at the cove and grasped her amulet as it pulsed gently against her heart.

It seemed that she got to live after all.

Epilogue

KEELIN GRASPED THE phone tightly in her hands and stared out across the fields towards the cove.

"Keelin, is that you?" Margaret's voice sounded tiny across the airwaves.

"It is, I'm here, Mom," Keelin said, and reached down to scratch Ronan's head.

"I haven't heard from you in almost two weeks. I was about to send out the guards," Margaret said stiffly.

"I know, I'm so sorry that I worried you, Mom. A lot has been going on." Keelin wondered where to begin. It wouldn't be right to attack her mother about Colin and Aislinn and she wasn't sure just how much she wanted to get into her newfound healing powers. She already knew how Margaret felt about those. With a sigh, she focused on the blue waters of the cove.

"You're staying, aren't you?" Margaret said. Keelin held the phone away from her face and stared at it in awe.

"Yes, I am. I…I need to be here, Mom."

Silence greeted her for a moment. Keelin heard her mother sigh.

"How's Fiona?"

"She's good, she needs me though. She's all alone here," Keelin said.

"But what about me? I'll be all alone here," Margaret said plaintively.

"No you won't. You have more friends than I do. You can always come back, you know," Keelin said.

"No, I don't suppose that I can," Margaret said definitively.

"Well, I hope that you will soon," Keelin said as she grinned down at the sparkling ring on her finger. Glancing up, she saw her new life walking over the fields to her, the dogs yipping at his feet. "I've met someone."

"Well, a summer fling certainly isn't worthy of me flying across the pond to Ireland, Keelin Grainne," Margaret said.

"Mom. He's it. He's everything," Keelin whispered.

Silence greeted her again and Keelin felt her heart drop in her chest. Maybe she was asking too much of her mother.

"Well, then, of course I will come. No man will ever live up to my daughter, but I will have to at least meet this man before you marry him. Now, tell me everything,"

Margaret said briskly, and Keelin felt a smile break over her face.

Flynn reached her and brought her hand with the ring to his lips. Her eyes shining, Keelin said, "You'll love him, Mom. He owns fifteen restaurants up and down the coast." Laughing, she leaned in to kiss Flynn and settled happily into her future.

An excerpt from Wild Irish Eyes: Book 2 in the Mystic Cove Series featuring Cait Gallagher:

Chapter One

CAIT GALLAGHER HUMMED along to the traditional Irish music that played softly through the speakers hidden deep in the corners of the pub that she owned in Grace's Cove, a small village set on the shores of Southern Ireland. Cait admired the gleam of the dark wood that accented all of her whimsical Irish décor as she wiped down a table. Content, and happy that the rehearsal dinner for Keelin and Flynn had gone so beautifully, Cait let her guard down and set her mind to wander.

"I bet she's good in bed. She's so tiny that I could throw her over my shoulder and drag her out of here."

Cait straightened as Patrick's voice shot through her mind. Forcing herself to keep all emotion from her face, she bent to wipe the table once more before turning towards the bar where Patrick, her new bartender, cleaned glasses in the new glass cleaner she had just purchased. Even if she couldn't read minds, the hunger she saw in young Patrick's eyes was unmistakable. He blushed when Cait glanced his way and, dipping his head, he focused on the task at hand. Cait blew out a small breath and ran a hand through her short, curly mop of hair. At just over five feet tall, Cait was indeed tiny. A slim frame, short hair, and greenish-gold eyes completed the package and often had her being mistaken for a little girl. Those who knew her never made that mistake. As a pub owner, Cait had a commanding presence, a rigid backbone, and a healthy dose of risk-taking. She'd been known to break up more than her fair share of brawls. Typically though, it took little more than her raised voice to stop an argument in its tracks.

Cait kept an eye on Patrick as she moved around the pub. A recent hire, he was just eighteen years old and full of testosterone and angst. With his dark hair and gray eyes, Cait imagined that he had already cajoled more than one girl into his bed. Smiling, she shook her head at the urgency of youth and reminded herself to keep her mental shields up, as she would probably hear more than she needed to from Patrick if she wasn't careful. Cait shot him a friendly smile as she ducked under the pass-through behind the long wood bar that framed rows of glass shelves hung in front of a gilded mirror. Liquor bottles of all shapes and sizes clustered the shelves. Cait prided herself on stocking more than just the average fare and enjoyed offering a variety of alcohol choices. She bent to tuck her cleaning supplies beneath the counter. Turning, she slammed into Patrick's chest and stepped back involuntarily as he caged her with his arms.

Cait took a deep breath as her pulse picked up its pace. Blowing out her breath, she met Patrick's eyes.

"I think about you. A lot." Patrick's words sent an involuntary shudder through Cait and she realized that maybe she should have listened a little more closely to Patrick's thoughts. Allowing her shields to drop, Cait did a quick scan of Patrick's mind. She breathed a sigh of relief as she found a healthy dose of lust but no intent to harm. Cait reached up and patted Patrick's arm.

"Patrick, I'm almost ten years older than you. While I'm flattered, you need to find a woman your own age to date." Cait smiled gently at him. She gasped as he wrapped his arms around her and pressed a passionate kiss to her lips. Cait let out a soft squeak before she contemplated how to break the kiss without bruising his fragile ego.

"What's going on here?"

A voice sliced across the pub and Cait tried not to groan as Patrick stepped hurriedly back from her. Cait knew that voice. Its owner had starred in more than one of her most decadent fantasies.

"Have I interrupted something?" Shane MacAuliffe stepped up to the bar and leaned casually against the railing as his brown eyes coolly assessed the situation. His lanky frame belied a whipcord strength that Cait had seen exhibited on several occasions.

"No, you haven't. Right, Patrick?" Cait turned and crossed her arms, staring down the young man. Patrick's cheeks turned pink and he ducked his head, nodding at the floor.

"Why don't you take the kitchen bin out and finish cleaning up in there?" Cait suggested, and Patrick nodded, not meeting her eyes. He ducked quickly beneath the pass-through and all but ran for the kitchen, the door swinging wildly behind him. Cait huffed out a sigh and turned to face Shane. She was dying to read his thoughts but her own code of honor prevented her from doing so. She'd have to deal with this like a regular person.

Cait allowed her eyes to scan Shane. His casually proper attire was something that she knew he took time with, just as she knew that he drove into Dublin for his haircuts. His blond hair and stubborn jaw made him an attractive, if not an interesting man to look at. The unofficial mayor of Grace's Cove, Shane owned more than half of the commercial real estate buildings, including the one that housed her pub. Still, that didn't mean it was okay for him be here after hours, Cait thought. Deciding to take the offensive, she glared at him.

"And what are you doing, sneaking in here after hours?"

Shane raised an eyebrow at her and Cait was startled to see anger lying beneath the cool surface of his calm façade.

"I own the place, remember?"

Cait blew out a breath and turned to finish cleaning the glasses. The task gave her something else to focus on and forced her to keep her mouth from saying something stupid like, "take me." Cait did a mental eye roll. She promised herself that one day she would get over this insatiable crush that she had on her landlord.

"Yes, sir, I remember." Cait infused her words with bitter sarcasm. He always hated it when she called him *sir*.

"Knock it off. What are you doing messing with that kid? He's too young for you," Shane said bitterly as he ducked behind the bar and helped himself to a Harp.

"Make yourself at home, there," Cait said.

"Put it on my house account. Now, answer my question."

Cait finished washing her hands and dried them carefully on a bar rag that hung in front of her. Part of her was gleeful that Shane cared and part of her was infuriated that he thought that she was too old for Patrick.

"My love life is my own. Thanks for asking though."

Cait gasped as Shane stepped towards her, pressing her small body back against the bar. She allowed her eyes to trail up his chest, past his clenched jaw, to where his deep brown eyes were murderous. It was so rare for Shane to show emotion like this that Cait found herself trembling against him.

"Your love life? You're sleeping with him? What kind of boss are you?"

Shock hit Cait at his words and a warm flush of anger and embarrassment shot through her.

Her voice shook and she skewered Shane with a glare.

"I'm the best kind of boss. One that knows what she wants and gets it. No matter what. And at this moment that would be you…leaving my pub. Now."

Shane took a deep breath and stepped back from her. Cait felt oddly bereft at the absence of his heat. She held his eyes as he nodded once at her and ducked beneath the pass-through.

"Excuse me, then. I'll just leave you to your business. I'm sure that Patrick can walk you home instead." Shane slammed through the front door and Cait brought her trembling head to the bar, allowing the smooth wood to cool the heat of her forehead. What had just happened? Cait needed a moment to breathe.

"Um, I'd be happy to walk you home."

Cait stayed where she was as Patrick's voice greeted her from across the room. If she knew her town, this would be the gossip on everyone's lips over breakfast tomorrow.

"No, thank you, Patrick. Come here, we need to talk."

Patrick walked to the other side of the bar and met her eyes, the naked hunger in his eyes softening her stance. Though Cait felt the pleasure of being wanted wash through her, she also knew that Shane was right. Patrick was not only too young for her, but he was also her employee.

She pulled out two shot glasses and filled them with a splash of Tullamore Dew. She slid one across to Patrick.

"Here's the deal, Patrick. I'm flattered that you are attracted to me. But, at your age, you'll find someone else in under a week. And you should…you should be out testing the waters and seeing what you do and don't like. Not only am I not the one for you, it also goes against my rules and my ethics to sleep with an employee. You do a good job here and I want to keep you on. But, I'm going to have to ask you never to make a pass at me again. Do you think that you can handle that?" Cait said firmly, her eyes never wavering from the young man's face. Patrick took a deep breath and nodded once before breaking into a smile.

"So, we're okay?"

Cait smiled at him and held up her shot glass. "Slàinte." They clinked glasses and she allowed the warm burn of the whiskey to slip down her throat. The heat only seemed to fuel her anger at Shane but she kept a cool demeanor as she and Patrick chatted about the rehearsal dinner they'd hosted at the pub earlier that evening. Cait went around and flicked off lights and tried not to think about why Shane had come to the pub tonight. Instead, she thought about Keelin and Flynn's wedding tomorrow. Cait was going solo as she was a bridesmaid in the wedding, but that didn't mean she wouldn't be able to mingle with the guests. Knowing that Flynn owned restaurants across Ireland had led Cait to hope that maybe she'd meet a new man, one not ensconced in Grace's Cove. One…that wasn't Shane. With a sigh, she ushered Patrick from the pub and locked the door behind her, pocketing her keys smoothly.

Her small flat was only a few blocks away and made her commute convenient though she often wished that she wasn't so accessible to all of her employees. Cait supposed that that was the drawback of owning your own business. She laughed at herself as she walked the quiet street towards her building. She loved owning a pub in Grace's Cove. Rumored to be a mystical town, the cove drew curiosity seekers from around the world. Tourism was a big business in Grace's Cove and Gallagher's Pub was at the heart of it. So what if people though the cove was enchanted? They wouldn't be far wrong, Cait thought. Rumors held that Grace O'Malley had protected it as her last resting place and that very few were allowed to enter the cove without being harmed. Whispers of powers passed down through Grace's bloodline heightened the reputation of the town. It was good for business and business was booming.

She wouldn't change it for the world, Cait thought, and smiled at the sleepy town.

Author's Note

On a warm, sunny day last September, my husband and I hiked up The Saint's Path located on Mt. Brandon in Dingle, Ireland. The Stations of the Cross lined the path and led to the highest point of the peninsula. At the top, the winds were fierce and the view almost heartbreaking in its staunch beauty.

Days later, I awoke to the bells of the Christchurch Cathedral in Dublin, in a lovely hotel room. A dream tugged at my mind. So powerful, so insistent, that for the first time in my life, I was compelled to write my dream down, worried that I would lose the threads of the story that had captivated me in my sleep.

Over the last few days of our trip, I babbled incessantly to my ever-patient husband as he politely listened to me play with characters and plot.

Soon, my dream had expanded from one book into a five book series.

Sometimes, you just have to follow that moment. That brief hint of inspiration that lights you up inside. That…something…that keeps niggling at your brain. The Mystic Cove books are those stories. The ones that I think about when I'm doing yoga or in the yard playing with my dogs. The ones that make me ache to return to the shores of Dingle and spend many a day soaking up the beauty and charm that the small village has to offer.

Thank you for taking part in my world, I hope that you enjoy it.

Please consider leaving a review online. It helps other readers to take a chance on my stories.

As always, you can reach me at omalley.tricia@gmail.com or feel free to visit my website at triciaomalley.com.

You can sign up for new releases here http://eepurl.com/1LAiz.

Author's Acknowledgement

First, and foremost, I would like to thank my husband for his unending support as I pursue this wildly creative career of being an author. It isn't easy to watch someone follow the creative path, and uncertainties are rampant. Josh, thanks for being my rock.

I'd like to thank my family and friends for their constant support and all of my beta readers for their excellent feedback.

Thanks to Emily Nemchick for her excellent editing services and to Alchemy Book Covers for their stunning cover designs.

And last, but never least, my two constant companions as I struggle through words on my computer each day - Briggs and Blue.

Made in the USA
Lexington, KY
02 August 2017